THE OTHER SIDE OF YES

A Feel-Good Romantic Comedy For The Sceptic

BELLYDANCING AND BEYOND SERIES

KERRIE NOOR

CONTENTS

In another life I was known as Janice, a student belly dancer living in Norwich, ignored and undesired.

I cleaned tables in my ex-husband's cafe and cooked him meals he didn't want; my pelvis, my womanhood, lay dormant, outcast and unused. I was a woman wishing her life away and I thought belly dancing was the answer.

We wanted children, but they never appeared. I told myself we wanted the same things and almost believed it. Until one day I walked into the café and there, bent over a table, was my husband like a dog on heat, and *her* screaming like a banshee, her chipped stiletto heels pointing at the sky.

That was that.

Twenty-one years of marriage wiped away with just one glance of my husband's naked pimply flesh pulsating to *Relax* by Frankie goes to Hollywood.

I remember sitting in our lounge staring at his Christmas presents waiting to be wrapped. On the table was the Christmas tree, candles and cards from some of the customers. I looked at his empty chair, the chair where he sat flicking his cigarette ash everywhere but in an ashtray and wondered why it had taken me so long.

Like my old granddad used to say, "Never stay where the pencil does not fit."

So with my coin belt and Hassam Ramzy CDs, and my new belly dancing name, I moped my way to Scotland, as far from the stiletto heel-wearer as possible.

Nefertiti was going to find a better life.

Chapter One

MR FINLAY'S SOCKS

Not every girl wants a doll

Sheryl

I was sitting in the garden watching Baby Bea play, while Mum relived the joy of seeing Mr Finlay's stiff socks.

Why she would remember I have no idea — she's never cleaned in her life. My mum — Beatrice — has as much idea of cleaning for a living as the Pope has of a hen night. She doesn't even do her own laundry; she leaves it for me or her on/off partner, George. Apparently living in a wheelchair makes emptying a washing machine impossible.

Cleaning for the likes of Mr Finlay is a memory burned in *my* head, sorting through his smalls was best done with gloves, in poor lighting, while holding my breath. He had prunes with everything and liked to get the "most out of his underwear" with a sniff and throw test, which meant wearing his socks until they stood up on their own then tossing in the vague direction of the laundry basket. Mr Finlay's sense of smell was as buggered as my post pregnancy pelvis, you'd only have to open the fridge to testify to that and it was one of the few things Mum and I agreed on.

Mum and I had reached a turning point in our so-called relationship, a turning point lubricated by red wine and Baby Bea, my delicious daughter. Nagging is the furthest thing from my mother's mind when

Baby Bea is about. Her face lights up, sometimes she even laughs, with a "thank you for bringing her into the world" look at me.

It's enough to make me want to visit more.

We had just polished off a bottle of red and were waiting for Steven to pick Baby Bea and me up when Mr Finlay's hygiene became a discussion point.

Mum, her face a healthy sun and red wine flush, was dressing an old doll she had sourced from the Red Cross shop which Baby Bea had as much interest in as the six o'clock news. She was too fascinated by Puss, Mum's cat.

"That Mr Finlay had no shame," said Mum, see-sawing a bonnet for a golf ball size head onto a head the size of a football. "But then he was always a bit of a minger."

I stared at Mum. The last time she said minger, I was in short socks and wore vest Dad was still alive and the only reason she said it was to get his attention.

"Yes," she said, "a real minger, his smalls were as toxic as nuclear waste."

"Mum, the only smalls you've ever sorted is the change in your purse."

"Pity the poor ambulance man that finds him on the floor." Mum attempted a more prolonged stretch and hold motion with the bonnet. "They'll have to scrape him off with a spade."

"Mum!"

"What?"

"That bonnet is never going to fit on that head."

Baby Bea made a grab for Puss.

Puss escaped with a skid.

Mum tossed the doll, minus bonnet, across to Baby Bea.

The doll landed with a thud by her feet, its cotton-stuffed limbs spread out like a starfish.

Baby Bea burst into tears.

"That's Nefertiti's biggest fear," said Mum.

"You mean Neff," I said, moving towards my daughter.

Mum looked at me.

"What? She likes to be called Neff."

"First I've heard of it. I mean, it's hardly regal, is it?"

"That's what living in Lochgilphead does to you. No one gives a toss about that sort of thing here and who wants to have "Nefertiti" shouted out across the GP waiting room? In fact I think that's what made her give into the whole "just call me Neff" thing."

Mum sniffed.

"And when has she ever seen Mr Finlay's socks, anyway?"

Baby Bea picked up the doll and hurled it at Puss.

Puss made a dash for cover under a hydrangea bush.

"Not the socks," said Mum. "To be found by the ambulance man…"

"I see." But I was still confused.

"…Her body letting her down," Mum added, "in the sort of position even a porn star wouldn't want to be seen in. Especially with her underwear, well, not at its best."

I picked up Baby Bea and the doll.

Baby Bea pushed the doll away.

"But that's what the paramedics are there for," I said. "To deal with bodies letting you down. They've probably seen more minging underwear than I've seen dirty nappies."

"Don't say that word, Sheryl!"

"What?"

"It a dreadful word."

"But you just said it…" I gave up, and plonked down beside her, Baby Bea in my lap.

Mum stretched out her arms and Baby Bea, doll forgotten, tumbled into her lap with a giggle. "Nefertiti…I mean, Neff, dreads the ambulance folk spreading soiled underwear rumours in the Co-op," she said.

"I wouldn't worry, those ambulance folk are sworn to secrecy," I said. "Confidentiality and all that. They'd have their tongues cut off and feed to the sausage factories if they said anything."

Mum threw me another "don't be ridiculous" look and then with an expert Baby Bea jiggle said, "Neff fears the bagging up of her things like yesterday's newspapers."

"I think you'll find it's the relatives who do that."

"Sent to the Red Cross shop for people like Ms Frasier to rummage through."

Mum always brought up Ms Frasier when exasperated, they had the sort of "love to prove each other wrong'" relationship which was worth watching as long as you didn't get involved. Ms Frasier had spent "her best years'" in the Outback and had a passion for second-hand shops or "Op shops' as she calls them. She's never out of the Red Cross Shop, pulling shirts and ties off the rack, reminiscing about the "poor dear departed, last seen only weeks ago, as fit as a Mallee bull". And no matter how many times she's asked what her first name is, Ms Frasier never replies. Mum recons she fancies herself as Lochgilphead's Columbo, while those in the Red Cross calls her Inspector Morse – but behind her back.

"...and for once I agree," said Mum. "The last thing I want is my life reduced to underwear and false teeth shoved into a garbage bag."

'I thought you didn't care?" I said. "That you wanted to be cremated."

Chapter Two

FOOT FUNGUS AND SEX

"If you must" is not the same as saying "Yes"

Sheryl

My legs were in the air, Steven was giving his all, and the only thing I could think of was, *all that fucking fungal cream and still my toenails look like a hawk's talons.* I had spent a fortune on that stuff, for what? Old piano key toenails as thick as tomb stones?

Not that I'm vain or anything but I do have a dread of dying with toe nails that make peoples' skin crawl. Toenails that can't be hidden with nail vanish...And don't get me started on skid marks.

I guess that's what caring for old folk can do to you.

I guess that's what listening to your mother can do to you.

All Mum's talk of ambulance men and soiled underwear was playing on my mind. Not the best thing to think of when you're trying to sound like a porn star, con your husband into thinking you're having the time of your life, he's the stud of the year, and that you've never had it so good.

Steven, with no idea about my feet issues, rolled off with a satisfied customer and a "you enjoyed it too" smile.

Not that Steven is a smug person, he does his best to please, and I do my best, even while glaring at my toes, to sound like he has. He deserves it. He listened to me all night as I ranted about Mum, ambulance men and underwear; he always did when I came home from Mum's.

He's an easy going man, is Steven. The sort you'd trust your passwords with, the type of guy you could safely hand over your credit cards and say, "Get me £20." He's a dream husband, too. He takes his turn to get out of bed to see to Baby Bea, he brings home a pint of milk when I ask – and it's always the right kind. In fact, he knows everything I like when it comes to filling the fridge. And yet when it comes to sex, he's just like every man I have been with.

He just doesn't understand the meaning of "I'm knackered" and he rarely gives up.

I usually give in, I know I won't get peace until I do and I find a healthy dose of "yes, yes, *yes!*" works wonders. It spurs him on to the finish line, like a whip with a race horse. Pre Baby Bea days this was all a piece of piss, my body was as quick to respond as a wasp sting, usually with a juicy "yippee". Giving birth changed all that, it really stuffed up my libido, now my "yippees" are as hard to find as a decent babysitter. Getting in the mood for me is as easy as stopping a Baby Bea tantrum. After the birth it took months for my equipment to return to "business as usual", but I often can't be bothered.

Not the sort of thing you can tell a husband who brings you coffee in bed, and rubs your back.

Nowadays I not only prayed for a quickie, I let rip, to spur him on.

Within minutes he was dosing, deep breathing the sort of sperm-well-spent kind. I sat up, walked to the bathroom, pulled on the light, and stared at my toenails – *fucking useless cream.*

Chapter Three

THONGS AND DUREX

The end of Sellotape is as hard to find as a man who uses Durex

Sheryl

A few days later I walked into Mum's kitchen to find Ms Frasier and Mum talking over a coffee like old buddies, which they always did, until Ms Frasier started on the Australian slang. That usually leads to a full-on sermon about the joys of Australia, a sermon Mum heard so many times she could write it down word for word. Ms Frasier comes out with the most insane things, usually about her time in the Australian Army – decades ago, when TVs had four channels and cars four gears (another favourite line of hers).

No one ever mentions Australia when they see her, not without regretting it, most shut up, wait for the tidal wave to die down.

Mum, however, tended to rise to the bait quicker than a snapper on the scent of a squid, reminding Ms Frasier just how far "Australia is from Scotland" and, "Who the hell do you think made the place? The Chinese?" At which point Ms Frasier would point out how "the Chinese did in fact make Australia great – just look at the dim sum," shutting Mum up quicker than a clam.

Mum's always been too pissed off to ask what a dim sum is, let alone listen to Ms Frasier's description of "the best bite-size takeaway you could get. They take the dipping of soy sauce to a whole new level."

On this warm summer's day, Steven and Baby Bea were in the garden and I, having decided to give an airing to the said toenails, appeared in flip flops – or as Ms Frasier reminded me, "thongs".

I waited for Mum to make some sort of uncomfortable underwear joke but this time she said nothing. She was in one of her rare listening modes, Mrs Frasier was talking McTaggart.

Before lockdown Mum and Ms Frasier bonded over a demonstration that brought down McTaggart, a councillor who had been a councillor since I was in school.

McTaggart or The Maggot as some called him had plans to close the library and set up a pop-up version in the community centre, where the Wall of Gratitude resided – a concertina wall that appeared now and then with photos of people who the community should be grateful for. Despite opposition on a par with a peace-rally, McTaggart had arranged a demonstration using the Wall of Gratitude, along with cheap-as-chips wine and out-of-date cheese with (according to Ms Frasier) the green bits removed.

Mum and Ms Frasier made counter plans.

Mum, using more egg boxes than an egg factory, camouflaged herself as a tombstone, (Ms Frasier's idea, although I can't remember why) and, along with a birthday party of Under Fives, created chaos. The mass destruction of the Wall of Gratitude accompanied any plans for a pop up library.

Ms Frasier always insisted that Mum was pivotal to the saving of the library, which left Mum in the position of putting up with Ms Frasier, in a teeth-gritting sort of way.

Today, Ms Frasier was talking about garbage bags. The sort that end up outside the Red Cross shop all weekend, waiting for it to open. The sort that Mr McTaggart complained about in a sniffy letter in the complaints section of the local newspaper.

"Everyone dumps their stuff there despite the sign saying not to," said Ms Frasier. "Someone pops their clogs and the next thing is, all their smalls and bric-a-brac are dumped like a bag of cat litter and–"

"You're not dumping mine, are you, George?" shouted Mum.

"What?" he called back?

George was in the living room doing man's stuff with Mum's TV. He practically lived with my mum, although his toiletries were kept out of sight in the bathroom.

"I'm talking about the Red Cross shop."

"That place?" said George's voice. "They're fed up turning up on a Monday morning to find bags of stuff, all wet with rain."

"Exactly what The Maggot wrote," said Ms Frasier.

"Yes, but you're not going to do that, are you?" Mum yelled at George.

George appeared at the door. "Some aren't even tied up properly," he said, with an "is she still here" nod at Ms Frasier. "Not a decent knot between them."

"Bugger all Durex," muttered Ms Frasier.

"We use the word Sellotape in this country." Mum sniffed.

McTaggart forgotten, Ms Frasier began to talk of her time volunteering in an Op shop in Australia. "There was always an influx of stuffed garbage bags after a death, suddenly you're going through some stranger's past, decades of accumulation." She sighed. "Not to mention the clothes, we got loads – even smalls and bathers...Who would want to wear used bathers?"

"Swimsuits." Mum sighed "And they are washed, you know – on a 90 degree cycle, so I am reliably informed."

"No one is poor enough to wear second-hand bathers," said Ms Frasier. "Apart from the homeless, I suppose, but what are they going to do with them?"

"I've never seen a homeless person in Lochgilphead," said Mum.

"It makes you think," said Ms Frasier.

"About what?"

"Your life ending up in a garbage bag, with folk like The Maggot complaining."

"There is more to life than bric-a-brac." George cast eye across Mum's heaving shelves.

"Don't you think about dying?" Ms Frasier asked.

"Not really." Mum was beginning to look irritated, she had that "where did I put the wine" look.

"Wine?" George offered.

Mum's face softened as she watched him pull out a bottle of Co-op Finest red and began to pour.

"All this stuff," Ms Frasier gestured towards Mum's shelves, "who's gonna sort it when you're gone?"

"Exactly," said George.

"Sheryl." Mum threw George a dirty look.

I looked at her with a "Me?"

"And her sister."

George handed her a glass.

"And George, of course."

"Don't look at me," said George, winking at me. "I'd burn the lot."

"I saw that wink," snapped Mum.

"All that graveyard nonsense." Ms Frasier just carried on. "The Aborigines don't believe in tombstones."

Mum sipped her wine. "They're a bit out of date here too."

"Mum wants to be cremated," I said.

"I merely talked about it..." She stopped, catching sight of my toe nails.

Ms Frasier's eyes followed Mum's.

"You can get cream for that," said Mum.

"Pff," said Ms Frasier. "That stuff is like hand, neck, eye, foot cream. None work, they just make the bathroom look like a spa."

"I do like my toiletries matching," I muttered.

"You'll need to go to the doctor's," said Mum.

"I'm not going to the doctor's about toenails."

"What if you knocked over by a bus?" said Ms Frasier.

Mum turned back to me. "Told you not to paint them."

"I used to paint yours," I said.

"Only on special occasions, not all the time."

"When my pal went through The Change, her toenails turned black," said Ms Frasier.

Mum flashed a *maybe it's The Change* look at me.

"It's not The Change," I snapped. "I'm just over forty."

"Forty-three," said Mum.

"Two, Mother...I'm forty-two."

"Still, that's when it all starts. They call it pre something," said Mum.

"Pre-menopausal, And I am not friggin' pre-menopausal, I'm still feeding Baby Bea."

"Yes, well. You know my thoughts on that."

I rolled my eyes at George; he threw me a commiserations look. "Sheryl knows what she's doing, luv," he said.

"I told my pal to try soya milk for The Change." Ms Frasier looked at my feet. "And tea tree oil for the feet."

"And who is this pal?" I asked.

"Did she listen?" said Ms Frasier. "Insisted on going to the doctor's, came back with a prescription for HRT and some paint for her toenails. Her feet never saw sandals for years. But she did end up with smooth skin." She took a large mouthful of Co-op Finest and swallowed. "Improved things in bed too." She turned to me. "Rampant as a kangaroo."

"Rabbit," said Mum.

"Does this pal have a name?" said George.

"Tea tree oil is all the rage in Australia. The Aborigines use it."

George, with a bored look, headed back to his TV.

"Tell me when the cricket is on," Mum called.

He stopped at the doorway. "You hate the cricket."

Mum gestured towards Ms Frasier. "Not the one day cricket."

"Oh I see…" George looked at me. "Should be on in a minute, then."

"Who's playing?" Ms Frasier asked.

"Australia," said George.

Ms Frasier's face lit up.

"Shit," muttered Mum.

Chapter Four

THE WIFE

You can't put a young vagina on an old pelvis.

Sheryl

A few days later I walked into The Taj Mahal, Lochgilphead's Indian restaurant, and locally known as "The Taj".

Lochgilphead is a one horse, one bike, one main street, town with one Chinese takeaway (no dim sim), three closed pubs, one fish and chip shop, run by Gordon who has an ongoing feud with Jason the fishmonger, and The Taj. The Taj is tiny and has been there since the seventies and up until lockdown the decor had never changed. Walking into that place was like walking into a sit com, most people joked about it with affection. I certainly did. But there was something reassuring about ordering a pakora surrounded by the same wall paper as your gran's, knowing what you were going to order, but taking your time about ordering it.

Neff started working in The Taj a few years before lockdown, and she took to it like my mum took to Baby Bea – as if it were as natural for her to take an order and pack a takeaway as it was for Ms Frasier to curse in Australian slang. She moaned like crazy, though, especially about the deliveries, according to her it always rained the moment she walked out the door. But she never looked happier, even when Tenzam and The Chef spoke in Bangla and she had no idea what they were saying. They always give her leftovers, too, which she took home to share with The Bag Lady, who lived in her garden.

Neff always said she worked there for the money, and that Tenzam would be lost without her. Ms Frasier said Neff did it because she felt needed, while my mum thought it was for the leftovers – but only after a few wines and she'd fallen out with George. Me, I think that the restaurant brought it out the mother in Neff. My mum laughed her head off when I said that, she said Neff was as motherly as a sea horse.

On the other hand, Steven said, "Anyone who not only allows a bag lady to live in her garden but teaches her to belly dance definitely has a story to tell."

He reckoned there was at least one book in her, something that lit up Neff 's face when he mentioned it. Neff looked as much like an author as a street lamp to me – not that I'd tell her that. I didn't need to; The Roadworks Man did it, and more. "If Neff's stories are anything like her driving then she should stick to serving curries," he'd announce cheerfully.

The Roadworks Man lives on his own in a flat above The Taj and practically lives in the restaurant which no one seems to mind, apart from Neff.

The Roadworks Man a man of habit arrived every night at the same time, and sat at the same seat. He'd spend ages staring at the menu, grinding Tenzam's patience into the ground only to order the same thing with a casual toss of the menu. Until Tenzam came up the "staff curry"; a plan that made The Roadworks Man feel so special he ate anything they put in front of him from weird-looking vegetables to fish heads.

Neff claimed he interfered with her customer banter, making comments and suggestions that according to her no one wanted to hear. He, in turn, criticised her banter, claiming no one wanted to hear her belly dancing music or her belly-dancing "pelvis talk." Which was a total exaggeration as it was Tenzam who chose the music and folk were so used Neff's pelvic talk they just switched off.

The Roadworks Man, a true Lochgilphead local knew just about every out-of-the- way address you could think of, being that he'd worked on the roads since he could vote.

When Neff first started, she sniffed at his directions until one dark night she set out with her sat nav to find some hidden farm and emerged hours later, drenched, cross and silent. The funny thing was The Roadworks Man said nothing, not one "I told you so", but Tenzam did, and from then on insisted on Neff taking The Roadworks Man with her whenever a new address appeared.

The Taj had been 'renovated' since lockdown. Looking pretty smart with clean white walls, posh recess downlighting and chairs that actually seemed comfortable. Even Tenzam looked smarter. It was as if he'd grown an inch, there was a pep in his step and a grin that lit up his face like he had won the lottery.

'How are you?" he asked me now, and before I could answer added, "Just waiting on Neff." He looked out the window. "We have a few deliveries."

I peered at the menu and, pointlessly, read it.

Tenzam waited with stoical patience, pen and pad poised.

I ordered our usual.

Tenzam nodded, like I was ordering for the first time, then ripped the ticket off his pad.

"Don't know why I read the menu." I laughed. "I always order the same."

He beamed at me then headed for the kitchen.

I was just in the middle of reading the ingredients of a Jalfrezi, idly wondering if I could repeat such a thing at home when Neff appeared, looking frazzled and wet, The Roadworks Man behind her. He threw me an 'I've been to hell and back" look.

There had been an on/off downpour and it seemed they were caught in it.

Neff huffed big time.

"I told you to mind the pot hole," The Roadworks Man said, dragging his usual seat from under his usual table.

"And as I said, I already knew." Neff marched behind the counter.

"Find that hard to believe the way you rattled over it."

"I didn't rattle. I slowed down,' said Neff.

"No you didn't."

"I did too, I put it in third."

The Roadworks Man lifted the menu. "If that was slowing down then I'm a pakora." He flicked the menu open like a newspaper. "I am never getting in a car with you again."

"That's a relief." muttered Neff.

The Roadworks Man slapped the menu on the table. "You drive like a maniac."

Neff opened the till. "You navigate like a maniac."

"Your driving is a danger to others."

Neff emptied a money bag into the till with an exaggerated clatter. "There is nothing wrong with my driving."

"Your driving," said The Roadworks Man, "would curdle a dip."

"Don't be ridiculous. My dips always arrive safe and sound." Neff shut the till with a slam.

Tenzam appeared. "Fried rice or..." He eyed The Roadworks Man's protruding stomach "...perhaps, boiled."

"I'd rather a beer after her driving," said The Roadworks Man.

Neff pulled a bottle of Cobra from the fridge and with a glare at The Roadworks Man opened the bottle and sat it on the counter.

The Roadworks Man looked at the bottle and didn't move.

"No need to worry," said Tenzam.

The Roadworks Man eyed the bottle. "Oh aye, forgot about that."

"Forgot about what?" asked Neff.

"That you'll not be doing deliveries after tonight," The Roadworks Man told her.

"Finally," Neff said. "They're a complete waste of time."

"No. I will be doing them," Tenzam explained. He slid the beer onto The Roadworks Man's table.

"You?" Neff stared at his back as he disappeared into the kitchen. She turned to me. "But he doesn't drive."

"He's got his license," said The Roadworks Man. "Did I not tell you?"

"I didn't even know he was learning..."

The Roadworks Man smiled. "I taught him."

Neff's face dropped. "Oh," she muttered.

At that point, Tenzam appeared with my carry-out. He placed it on the bench, and read the receipt: "One korma, one mixed pakora, one vegetable curry, two fried rice and a naan."

Neff threw him an "Is that absolutely necessary" look.

I was the only customer.

Tenzam chuckled, catching my eye, as The Roadworks Man began to expand on Tenzam's ability to drive, which according to him was the safest he had ever seen. "He listens." He gave Neff a pointed look. "And he takes directions."

Neff returned to her huffing, rearranging the pads and pens until The Roadworks Man began to talk of a *new arrival.*

"He wanted to learn before *she* arrived," he said.

Neff turned to Tenzam. "Who is *she?*"

Tenzam disappeared into the kitchen.

"His wife," said The Roadworks Man. "Did you not know?"

"I...No." Neff stopped. "I had no idea."

"Neither did I," I was about to say when The Roadworks Man turned to me. "Married for years, they're childhood sweethearts."

As he came back in the restaurant, Tenzam's mobile rang, and he started talking in Bangla.

"That's probably her on the phone now," said The Roadworks Man. "They've been on the phone every day, making arrangements. He's really excited."

"I did wonder why he was doing up the flat," muttered Neff.

"He's got family in Glasgow, you know," The Roadworks Man added.

Neff looked up with a glare. "I know that," she spat.

Chapter Five

THE NEW ARRIVAL

My name is Nefertiti but you can call me Neff.

Neff

So typical of Tenzam not to tell me and say he did. He's always done that, like he lives on another planet. The "I think therefore I say" planet.

He said I never listened, which is a complete load of bollocks. I always listened. Listening is my second name...my middle name...my first name. I am the listener of the century. In fact I could fill a friggin' stadium with the amount of people I have listened to.

Of course, Mavis disagreed. She said I have as much ability to listen as a deaf cat. But then that's the sort of comment I'd expect from her, she never liked cats, apart, that is, from my dear departed Puss.

There I was, drenched and dealing with that smart aleck Roadworks Man, just recovering from Tenzam's, "Now I'm a driver" bombshell when in walked Mavis like something out of LaLa Land. She had absolutely no intention of ordering. I could always tell, she never ordered without Lumpy, her other half. When she came in on her own it was to gloat, gloat and sometimes fish.

There was no fishing today though, just pure gloating with a little salt rubbing into *my* wounds.

"Is she here yet?" she asked with her favourite coquettish smile.

I threw her my best "really?" look. I wasn't going to let her know I was confused as hell.

"He's picking her up at the airport tomorrow morning," said The Roadworks Man.

Her? I still wasn't letting on.

"Who?" said Sheryl, like an owl.

"Oh I thought you said she was coming today," Mavis said.

She? Who's she? I thought, forcing a smile.

Then Tenzam appeared with an "I'm heading off" look, grabbing the restaurant car keys like he did it every day, and I couldn't help myself.

"You driving?" I said.

"Yes"

"Where?"

"Glasgow." He said it like he was wandering down to the Co-op for a packet of crisps.

I couldn't believe it, Glasgow is a two hour drive away, with heavy traffic and enough roundabouts to make a novice pee himself; a nightmare for any one used to driving in Lochgilphead. Lochgilphead has one roundabout the size of a wheel hub, no traffic lights and police you'd have a pint with if the pubs were open.

"You're going to Glasgow," I repeated.

"Of course."

"What? Now?"

"Yes I told you."

"So...you want me to close up then?"

Tenzam threw me his best sweet smile and nodded a yes. I could feel my blood pressure rise to boiling point. Then I stopped...*what the hell was wrong with me, why did I care if I was the last to know?* I tried to calm down while Tenzam put his bag in the restaurant's car and came back for a takeaway, which he could deliver on the way.

"Have a safe trip," I muttered.

Mavis stood there. She could read me like a TV page.

I threw her *my* best smile but she wasn't fooled, even when I asked if she was ordering. She coolly said she was waiting for Lumpy – who always had the ability to appear from nowhere right in the middle of a "Mavis is always right" sermon.

Turns out Tenzam not only has a wife but was going to pick her up – and everyone except me and Sheryl knew. Even the bus driver, and he doesn't even live here.

Mavis said that she had not only told me once, but several times throwing in her usual, "but you never listen." I told her that her idea of listening was ear wigging, which had The Roadworks Man snorting in his dhal. Lumpy arrived to back Mavis up to the hilt with, "I thought you took it pretty well."

"That's because you never told me," I snapped.

"They did, I was there," said The Roadworks Man, which was a complete lie.

"You mean you were ear wigging, which doesn't count as you always get it wrong."

"Do not," said The Roadworks Man.

"Do, too. You told me Tenzam was single."

"Oh. Forgot about that. Guess I picked his brother up wrong...Or was it The Chef?"

Mavis, Lumpy and The Roadworks Man stayed for way too long, eating their takeaways rather than taking them home. I finally got rid of them and was just about to cashed up when Mavis, only minutes from leaving the restaurant, phoned to see if I was alright?

"I'm in the middle of counting," I said. "Can I call you back?"

"I just wanted to know if you were ok." She said it in that annoying, concerned, way of hers.

"I'm counting..." I said, which was a complete waste of breath, she just carried on.

"I am sure Tenzam meant well," she said. "He probably didn't want to upset you."

"Me, upset, hardly."

"The last thing he'd want is one of your full-on sulks."

"I do *not* sulk. And why would I when I *so* hate deliveries. I'm friggin' glad he's driving and can do them. Let him sit in the car with that Roadworks Man and his so-called directions."

"Yes, but...he...may not need you any more...with a wife to help."

I stopped. I never thought of that. I stared about the restaurant; the pile of napkins I folded, listening to belly dancing music; the food left over for me and The Bag Lady.... "Pff, I'll be glad," I said.

Silence.

"Seriously," I added. "I'm sick of coming home stinking of curries."

"You said you liked the smell" said Mavis. Which was as true as her, "I told you so-s."

Chapter Six

THE SON OF RAMSES TWO

A cat by another name still prefers chicken to tinned food

Neff

When I arrived home that night The Bag Lady was sitting outside her teepee – cutlery and plates ready for the takeaway – warming her hands by the remains of a camp fire.

I was surprised to see her alone, as Betty was usually there. Betty stays with her son Shifty in The Argyll, the only pub in Lochgilphead. Shifty is the man who took my Rodger to the other side, who shops in the Co-op holding my ex's hand. And I have learnt to come to terms with it – well, you have to in a small town, where you bump into everyone and anyone, even at the GP surgery.

Betty, a woman too old to care what others think, likes to spend her evenings with The Bag Lady; in fact I had a portion of curry for her, as well.

The two women were way past the age of sitting cross-legged by a campfire and yet they did it. I often wondered about their past and what a great story it would make.

When she saw me, The Bag Lady gestured to The Son Of Ramses Two, who was peering down from my bedroom window.

"Something's eating that cat," she said.

I looked up to catch his "where the hell have you been," look, geared at me.

The Son Of Ramses Two was my new cat who, up to now, had been a strictly sleeping-by-the-fire sort of cat, aloof, distant and way too good for my bed, let alone The Bag Lady's tent. Then, a week ago. he took to my bed, hogging it like a limpet, like it was his and I should bugger off, or at least not move. And heaven forbid if I did, a mere cough had him glaring the sort of dirty look that could shame the Mafia.

He was like a bolder embedded to the mattress, as immovable as a wart on a foot.

I could lift him a thousand times from the bed and he would still find a way to sneak back onto it, and glare.

When I first got him, he was so up himself, he sniffed at his food, jolted away like it was electrified, then pushed it about with his paw. He was fussy about his food, perfecting a sniff and snooty stroll motion that had me spending a fortune on cat food. But yesterday he gulped down my leftover chicken and raced upstairs, almost tripping me up in the rush.

"He's been up there all day, even when I called," said The Bag Lady, peering into our takeaway and pulling out the boxes.

Not even a piece of chicken could entice The Son Of Ramses Two.

My old cat, Puss was a pushover compared to him.

She'd been terrified of Go Boy, the German Shepherd next door, who to be fair was getting on a bit. Once he started barking it would be hours before he'd stop and Puss spent those hours hiding. Not The Son Of Ramses Two. He strode the top of the fence tormenting Go Boy, and refused to leave until Jason, a sullen teenager, appeared shouting, "Simmer down, boy," and "That will do," followed by a smack over the head with a rolled up newspaper.

Puss died at the beginning of lockdown and I had refused to get another cat until The Son Of Ramses Two appeared looking like... well...Egyptian Royalty. The Bag Lady and I had been sitting in the hot tub at the time, celebrating a full moon with way too much gin, when he appeared from Puss's bush like God appearing to Moses. He eased himself on to the corner of the hot tub like it was his home, like he owned it lock, stock and smoking hot water, then looked at us as if we were intruding.

It was hard to believe that such a sleek cat had no home but apparently he didn't.

For a week I tried to ignore him parading around my garden, peering into my patio doors, staring me down, but that night as he sat erect like a statue, his grey silken fur glistening under the moonlight, it seemed as if I, like Moses, had been chosen.

Maybe it was the gin, but I felt honoured...

"I propose a toast," I'd said, and slurred, "The Son Of Ramses Two!"

The Bag Lady looked at me. "That's a mouthful."

"That cat is so royal he deserves a name that makes you sit up," I'd explained.

We both stared at the cat and The Son Of Ramses Two held our gaze like a snake hypnotising its prey.

"Regal personified," I said.

"It's a cat," muttered The Bag Lady.

"But what a cat," I said. "Besides, no one else around here has that name."

"Who would?" The Bag Lady had muttered again.

I plonked myself down next to The Bag Lady and sorted out my food.

"So he's gone to pick up his wife," said The Bag Lady, tipping her Jalfrezi onto her plate.

"You knew?"

"Mavis texted me, said you were a bit upset."

"Me, upset?" I tipped my dhal into a bowl, spilling half of it. "As if."

The Bag Lady ripped the naan in half and handed me mine.

My phone pinged.

Assuming it was Mavis reminding me yet again how many times she had told me about "the wife" I lifted it – to find it was Tenzam: *Can you work lunchtime? I won't be back 'til late,* followed by a line of smile emojis and one prayer pose at the end.

"Just as well I had nothing planned," I muttered.

The Bag Lady, with a mouthful of rice, eyed me.

"He won't be back 'til to tomorrow night," I said.

The Bag Lady nodded.

My phone pinged again: *Anything you want in Glasgow?*

"He wants to know if we want anything?"

The Bag Lady looked up at The Son Of Ramses. "How about one of those hot chickens from Morrisons, for himself."

I stared up at the window. "I can't eat with him staring," I said.

I went upstairs. The Son Of Ramses Two jumped from the window sill with a thud. I pulled the curtains then stared down at my cat circling my legs. I lifted him. He definitely felt heavier.

My phone pinged again: *Make it small, the car boot is full?* Another smile emoji.

As well as the back seat.

The Son Of Ramses Two jumped onto my bed and after a series of circles curled into a plump round ball. Maybe I could try a different cat food.

MENOPAUSE

Paranoia is a great storyteller

Sheryl

The nurse looked at my toes with a blank face.

"They are disgusting, aren't they?" I said.

"It's one toe."

"Still disgusting."

"It's one toe, a bit black, hardly disgusting."

"And what about that?" I gestured to my little toe.

"A bit of thickening, nothing to get upset about, I've seen worse on a doll."

"But I know where it leads. I've cleaned for Mr Finlay."

The nurse pulled a face. "It takes decades to get into that state." She looked at me, making my face flush red. She thrust a prescription at me. "Just use this and cover it with nail polish." She smiled. at me "For any sandal emergency."

I slid off my cardigan, fanning my face.

"Hot?"

"Just a little, it will go in a minute."

She threw me another nurse look. "How old are you?"

"What?"

She looked at the screen, whistling through her teeth. "I had no idea you'd reached your forties."

"I'm *just* forty one...two. Hardly forties."

"Maybe we should test your hormones."

"Why?"

She flicked though my files on the computer, with the sort of motherly fashion only a woman on the cusp of retirement could do.

She been a nurse since I could remember, in the days when the GP was a small room in a house. She was the district nurse back then, visiting folk like Mr Finlay. I had met her in his house many times, usually when she was giving him a lecture about not drinking and eating vegetables.

It was her I saw when I started on the pill, and when my mother was getting used to her wheelchair. She had even attended one of Nefertiti's free NHS belly dancing classes. Now she's a practice nurse in a slick GP surgery attached to the hospital, the sort of surgery barracked by an overworked receptionist and phone consultations.

"Forty is, well, forty." She turned to me. "When was your last period?"

"Before Baby Bea was born."

"You really must stop calling her that. She's not a baby any more. She's two."

"She likes it."

"You should have had a period by now."

"But I'm still feeding her."

"She's two."

"Not quite."

"Well yes, but she is walking."

"It helps her to sleep, and, well, I feel close."

"Well maybe that is why you haven't had any period."

A tear fell. .

"What's wrong now. Sheryl?"

"Don't know."

She handed me a tissue.

"I feel so emotional."

"Maybe you should wean her off and let yourself recover. Let things settle."

"I don't want to." I sniffed. "I work all day and, well, it makes me feel like a mother."

She peered over her glasses.

"Maybe I should..." I faltered. "Oh, I don't know."

"Let's do a few blood tests, check your hormones, shall we?"

"Hormones for what?"

"The Change."

"The change? Oh. "The Change". But I'm only... "I stopped. "Shit."

"Just to rule things out, make sure you know all is ok."

I blew my nose. "I just want to wear sandals again."

She patted my knee and pulled out a syringe.

Feeling a little dazed at the idea of The Change, I decided to visit Steven in the library. He's always so at home there, so confident, and I was hoping for some soothing reassurance – or at least a decent book on the subject of The Change.

I walked in to find him busy sorting out a selection of books. With a crisp stamp of a book he threw me an, "I'll be with you in a minute" look.

I didn't notice Neff or Mavis at first.

In fact I assumed the library would be empty apart from Ms Frasier; who tends to hog the newspaper table, breaking the silence with her intermittent, "Did you hear this?" to Steven.

The library was rarely open anyway. Despite lockdown having been and gone it was still sticking to the hardly open rules, promoting online eBooks and audio like crazy.

Passing Ms Frasier, engrossed in the latest 'The Scotsman', I moved to the shelves for a browse. I headed to the women's section, quickly passing books about pregnancy – the books Steven and I had poured over when I was expecting. I gazed over the titles about hormones, fertility, the goddess within, raising baby books, sex books, how to save a marriage books, painless period books, eating for moods books, finally stopping at "Owning Your Menopause", the first in a row of books about The Change.

I fingered the cover, slid it into my hand and was just about to feel sorry for myself when I caught sight of Neff at the next bookcase, staring at a line of Joanne Trollope, apparently deep in thought. Mavis was on the other side at the cosy murder and mystery section that spilled into grim Scottish crime novels. She peered over the top of the bookcase at Neff and whispered, "It's just a carry-out," then turned to me with a, "Hi, Sheryl."

Neff pulled "A Village Affair'" from the shelf, glanced at it, then slid it back with a tut. "People do sit in." She threw a look at me. "Don't they, Sheryl."

"Er... Yes?"

"You've sat in many times, haven't you?"

"Well, I..."

"And I like to think I give them more than their money's worth. Isn't that right, Sheryl?"

"Money's worth?" repeated Mavis.

"Yes, service with a sense of—"

Ms Frasier flicked a page with an "as if " tut.

Neff with a glare at Ms Frasier continued. "respectable banter."

Mavis looked at Neff like she was talking another language. "Folk go there for a decent korma not a standup routine."

"Shhh," whispered Steven from his desk.

"It's hardly a career," Mavis went on and Neff called her "offensive." Mavis called Neff "precious."

"Shh." Steven said. Louder.

Neff stared at the bookshelf with a downcast look. "My days in the takeaway are numbered."

"You don't know that," said Mavis.

"I can feel it in my waters."

"Stepping aside for another woman is not easy," said Ms Frasier.

"Bit dramatic," muttered Mavis, with a look at Ms Frasier.

"Did Tenzam actually say he didn't need you anymore?" I asked.

"I feel as needed as a wart," moaned Neff.

"Even a wart has its place," said Ms Frasier.

Mavis threw her another "have you been on the piss" look.

"Get a new haircut. That's what I'd do," said Ms Frasier.

"There's nothing wrong with my hair."

"It could do with an update," Mavis agreed.

Neff eyed Mavis' purple highlights until I could see both an insult brewing and Mavis bracing herself.

"Treat yourself." Ms Frasier nodded.

"It's hardly a treat if I am paying," said Neff.

"You can use your over sixties bus pass," suggested Mavis.

"I'd rather drive." Neff sniffed.

"It's free." Mavis reminded her.

"There are more important things than a free bus pass."

"Shh," said Steven, but he looked at me with a warm smile.

I smiled back.

"For the last few months you been going on about that bus pass," whispered Mavis. "How it's burning a hole in your purse."

"I think you'll find that was you," Neff snapped.

"You need your memory checked," Mavis hissed back.

"Mavis," said Neff. "You don't know everything, and reading an Iain Banks' novel doesn't make you an intellectual, merely a smart arse."

"You could have a snooze on the bus," I said. "No driving worries."

"I like driving," said Neff. She turned to Mavis. "And there's nothing wrong with my memory, I'm not over the hill yet."

"There's a place in Oban, half price for pensioners." Ms Frasier didn't look up.

Neff's face pinched tight. "Pensioner? Me?"

"And a free cappuccino." Ms Frasier turned a page. "Free Prosecco on Mondays, and cut price pedicures. Why not go for the full bhoona? Face mask, eyebrows, whip that moustache off–"

"Moustache?" screeched Neff.

"One look in the mirror and all your problems will fly out the window," Mavis added.

Neff was beginning to look like a cornered bull in a ring. "My problems are as non- existent as my moustache," she shouted.

Normally Steven would have read the Riot Act by now, asked them to leave. But not today. Catching sight of me with "Owning Your

Menopause" stopped him in his tracks. I slid the book onto the counter and threw him a weak smile, remembering when I was in labour and how wonderful he was, overcoming his fear of driving to follow behind the ambulance. There I was, dilating like a drug addict's pupil, frightened as fuck and he, according to the ambulance driver, "Stuck to us like shit on a shoe."

God it was reassuring.

I stared at 'Owning Your Menopause", watching as Steven stamped the inside, and realised I wanted it all again: another baby.

I yearned for it so badly I could feel my uterus weep.

Tears filled my eyes.

I couldn't get out of that place quick enough.

Chapter Eight

BABY BEA

Being old enough for a free bus pass comes to us all, and not using it doesn't make you younger

Sheryl

That night I stared at Baby Bea – who really *isn't* a baby any more, but a walking, talking, breathing, giggling little girl toddler with round tummy and dimpled smile – and ran my finger along the side of her temple. She was already asleep so I didn't need to do it, and yet I did. Her soft skin was just so delicious. I stared at her long lashes as they fluttered on her round baby cheeks and she pursed her lips with a sleepy sigh.

Maybe the nurse was wrong?

But I had been tearful lately.

A tear fell.

I did forget my lunch that day; and what was the other thing?

Shit.

Steven appeared. He slid his arm around my waist. "What's up?"

"Nothing."

"Nothing? Sheryl, you're crying."

"I am not."

"You are. What's up? It's not your toes again, is it? I told you to try Vicks VapoRub – it just takes time."

"It's not that. I just got some ointment from the nurse."

"Oh."

I sighed. "She thinks I might be going through The Change. That's why I got the book out."

He blinked.

"The menopause," I clarified.

"I know what it is." He slid his finger into baby Bea's palm. "But you're not even forty. Way too young."

"I'm forty- two. Almost."

"Oh yes, keep forgetting that you're a little older than me."

I looked at him.

"You don't look it," he added quickly.

"She called it my forties."

"It's only a number."

"And my periods have stopped."

"But you're breast feeding." Steven gripped me tighter. "I thought you had to be old for menopause."

"The Change is ageless," I muttered.

"Maybe you should start eating tofu."

I looked at him.

"The Japanese don't have hot flushes and they eat it all the time."

"You sound like my mother."

"Well, sometimes she's right. It comes from working with books."

"Yes, but you have to read them, which she doesn't, apart from the covers." I burst into tears.

"What wrong now?" he said.

"I don't know," I lied. Another tear fell.

"Tell me," he whispered.

"Today at the library when they were talking about driving I was thinking of you, how you drove behind the ambulance when I was in labour."

"Any father would have done that."

"But you were terrified of traffic." I sniffed.

"I wouldn't say that."

"Motorways made you sick and yet..." I burst into more tears. "You were so heroic."

"I hardly think—"

"I want to do it again." I sobbed.

Steven hugged me. "What?"

"Have another baby."

Steven rubbed my back.

"But how can I?" I wailed.

Steven sighed.

"I'm so tearful these days." I blew my nose. "Apparently it the first sign of low oestrogen."

"I hardly think—"

"I read it in that book."

"I did wonder why you were taking it out."

Feeling a bit like a tit I pulled away.

Steven turned me to face him and cupped my face in his hands. "You always get tearful. You cried watching Frozen." He kissed my nose. "You cry as easily as you laugh." And wiped a tear. "That's not a bad thing, is it?"

"But I'm forgetful."

"So am I." Steven shrugged. "That's what getting up at two in the morning to see to a toddler can do to you. Especially when you're up again at six."

Chapter Nine

THE BUS RIDE

I had been told to retire gracefully but I do things gracefully it's the belly dancer in me

Neff

I watched the bin lorry pull up at the car park opposite. It was the crack of dawn. The world was waking up and my stomach was like a glass of Alka-Seltzer.

I was sitting in a bus shelter, waiting for the bus, but I felt as if I was waiting for the dentist. I was as agitated as my first day at school, on edge, like I'd sculled a dozen expressos.

I don't know why Mavis thought I needed cheering up, just because she found me staring into the garden as if it were an abyss. *As if The Taj had ripped out a hole in my life.* I told her she was dramatic, which she claimed was *my* speciality and then suggested again a new look. "It always works for me," she said. "Well, that and a bit of how's your father with Lumpy." Mavis is one of those annoying friends that second guesses everything, puts two and two together and comes up with ten. She thought my reluctance to use my bus pass was an age thing and was quite happy to let me know that. (Not that I have seen her on the bus...)

The truth was that my last bus journey was as painful as a break up. In fact it was during a break up; I was coming back from Glasgow rejected and devastated. It was years ago now, back in the days when Rodger still lived with me.

I met Rodger after I had left my husband and although we never married I thought we were soulmates – forever holding hands until one of us hit the grave. He was in hospital recovering from a car accident and I'd spent the afternoon sitting by his bed, wanting desperately to touch him, but he kept pulling away. Then Shifty appeared and before I knew it *they* were holding hands.

I'd had no idea Rodger was in love with another man.

The journey home on the bus that day is a memory I'd rather forget. But this business at The Taj was bringing it all back.

"I feel rejected. Yet again," I told Mavis.

She looked at me like I was quoting Shakespeare in Gaelic and making a dog's dinner of it. "You just pack and deliver takeaways," she said. "Hardly the captain of a ship."

"Not that. It's just like that last bus ride, you know – when Rodger was in hospital."

Mavis stopped. "Oh I see." She turned to me with a soft look. "Would you like me to come with you?"

A soft look moves mountains and Mavis's touched something deep in me, pushed me to face my demons and accept that the only way to face them was on my own.

Easy to say before the deed. But this was what got me here, watching the bin men clutter along the pavement, and already missing my morning coffee. It's a good hour and a half drive on the bus, a long time for a bladder of a certain age. There was a time when my bladder could hold a keg of beer without a drip – even with a good sneeze – but not now. Not that I'd tell anyone.

Relax, I told myself, there is bugger all in your bladder, and when that didn't work I took a deep yoga inhale and let it out – nothing. I pressed my forefinger against a nostril, inhale, exhale, thumb to the other nostril, inhale, exhale.

I swear I saw the bin man stare.

He didn't look the sort that breathed for relaxation. He looked the sort who thought yoga was a type of yogurt and heavy breathing was something he did on top of a woman.

The bus pulled up.

The door slid open.

I attempted a casual 'jump on' and tripped.

I righted myself with a flustered, "Return to Oban!"

The driver stared at me with irritation and gestured to the card machine.

I fumbled with my card.

"Face up," he snapped.

I fumbled some more.

He tutted. "I said, face-up."

I looked at the three passengers already onboard; they stared out the window. So I fumbled again, my middle age technology quip nose-diving into the silence. The driver grabbed my card, flicked it over the machine, and with a surly, "Here," handed it back to me.

The bus lurched into first gear.

I stumbled into a seat.

"You can't sit there," he shouted.

I moved down the aisle.

"Or there.'

The three passengers stared at me like I was inebriated foreigner with possible signs of dementia.

"How about a friggin' sign?" I wanted to yell, then saw the sign and blushed.

The bus pulled into the next stop and a bottle-blonde bounced on.

"Isn't it cold!" she joked, expertly managing her sixty plus card.

The driver said nothing, started the bus, and she staggered to the front seat.

"You can't sit there," he hissed.

At which, she glanced at me and I at her...and contact was made.

A few hours, and several Proseccos later, I was at the bus stop for the return journey home, my bladder reassuringly empty.

I had spent the afternoon with a hairdresser who had been generous with the Prosecco, apparently the boss was away and as she had opened the bottle just for me, I *might* as well finish it.

As I was waiting, the bottle-blonde from the morning appeared. She looked at my hair and said, "Pensioner deal haircut?"

"Yes."

"I guess you get what you pay for." She sniffed as the bus pulled up.

The bus was full of high school students talking non-stop, until I stepped on. They stared at me like I was naked with an extra set of breasts. I threw them my best sober smile, and I liked to think they swallowed it. The bus driver certainly did.

"New hair?" he said with a big smile.

Some of the students laughed. I assumed it was because I looked amazing; I can't remember the last time I was so close to youth on mass. The banter was like another language and they, another species. They were so loud they drowned out Radio 2, even when the driver turned it up full blast.

A bumpy ride can fair put a drunk woman to sleep and I slept through most of it, my head fuzzy with memories of my time in front of the hairdresser's mirror. I was vaguely aware of the bus stopping and starting, high school students stumbling up the aisle, until the bus crashed to a stop and someone stumbled into my lap.

"Jesus Christ," snapped the bus driver as a sheep sauntered across the road.

The girl student lifted herself from my lap with a warm smile. As the boy behind took her hand, she caught my eye. "Love your hair."

"Thank you," I said.

"So bold."

"Thank you."

"My gran wouldn't be seen dead in pink."

"It's ok," shouted the boy to the driver. "We can get off here"

The girl threw me another smile, told me not to take any notice of what the others said, called me an inspiration.

I watched them jump from the bus, clasping hands, and shoving each other with playful pushes, laughing until the boy flung his arms around her. They stopped and kissed and were still going at it when the bus pulled away, leaving me alone with the bus driver and Gloria Gaynor singing on the radio: *I am what I am...*

"Oh to be that young again." The driver sounded strangely human.

He drove on, singing to himself, and I caught his face in the mirror. It was a picture of happiness.

Funny to think he was the same grumpy man of the morning, but maybe he was not a morning person. He sang louder and louder as we went down the road, past the sheep and their lambs. In fact, he forgot I was there and nearly missed my stop until I staggered up the aisle.

When I arrived home I didn't see my hair at first, I was too busy making it to the loo. Then I slid my hands under the tap and looked up at the mirror – and stopped. It dawned on my why the students hadn't looked directly at me; without a decent amount of Prosecco pink stiff hair looks really stupid.

They were trying not to laugh.

Chapter Ten

PINK HAIR

Riding a bus is hardly water-rafting up the Amazon, unless it the first time you've done it.

Neff

Mavis thought it was funny when I told her; she laughed so hard she was in tears. "You should write it all down. Makes a great story," she said. But that was *before* she saw my hair.

I was sitting in my living room with a scarf wrapped around my head at the time and Mavis was all ears, on the edge of her seat.

I was telling her about the hairdresser in Oban, a woman young enough to be my granddaughter, who looked at me as if my brain was as empty as a hot air balloon.

"She said pink was liberating."

"Pink?" Mavis repeated. "*Pink?* Isn't *pink* a bit Barbie doll?"

"Apparently not at my age. According to her I would find pink as liberating as, well, sex after the menopause."

"She said that?"

"Let's just say she alluded to the "after the menopause"."

Mavis looked unconvinced.

"She did give me a large Prosecco. Or two."

"I see."

"And on an empty stomach. I hadn't even had my morning coffee."

"Are you saying you were pissed in the hairdressers?"

"She said she knew me from my belly dancing days. That "I had given her a hen night to remember". Before my hair was washed and dried she topped me up again, and then when I told her all about Rodger—"

"You told her about Rodger?"

"Everyone tells hairdressers their secrets."

"I don't," said Mavis primly.

"She said, "You poor thing,", lifted the Prosecco again, looked at the bottom and said, "Here, have the rest, the boss is away all day"."

"So how much did you have, Neff?"

"Let's just say I had enough to enjoy Radio 1."

"Bloody hell."

"I told her to do her best."

"And did she?"

"There was I under a hair dryer, my toenails getting a seeing to, my finger nails a matching polish, a new me about to emerge."

"And did it?"

"When she lifted the dryer she took one look and opened another bottle. "On the house," she said. "The others in the salon were speechless.""

"A hairdresser's full, with nothing to say? I find that hard to believe." Mavis frowned.

"Then this morning I woke up to – this!" I pulled the scarf from my head.

"Jesus Christ!" Mavis yelped. "You caught the bus looking like that?"

"As I said, I'd had a few. Although I did wonder why that dipstick of a bus driver was suddenly kind to me. Even told me not to bother with my card."

"Fuck sake." Mavis stared at my head. "Did you pay for that?"

My face burned. "He even let me sit behind him. In the illegal seat."

"No wonder," said Mavis. "Shall I make a coffee?" She stared some more at my hair. "With sugar?"

Getting on a bus half cut is not something I had done for a while, decades if I'm honest – when I was young enough to look like a student myself.

"Riding a bus after a few is a completely different ball game," I said, "especially when you're old enough to be the driver's grandmother."

Mavis told me I was exaggerating, that bus drivers weren't that young and then she disappeared into my kitchen to find a bottle of something alcoholic. She had clearly given up on the coffee.

I followed her, lost in thought.

Mavis opened the fridge and gazed at the contents while I looked in the kitchen mirror, wondering if I could dye the great puff of pink that was now my hair, darker. *Maybe purple?*

"There is always a headscarf," Mavis said. She pulled a bottle of wine from the fridge and shut it with a slam, to find The Son Of Ramses Two behind the door, glaring at her. She jumped, almost dropping the wine bottle. "Must he do that?" She asked, gingerly walking around him.

I told Mavis he was regal, probably of Egyptian descent.

"He is a cat," she said, "and looking a little tubby."

The Son Of Ramses Two circled Mavis's legs.

I stared back at my hair as memories of Gloria Gaynor, and the singing bus driver came flooding in. I began to sing.

"What?" said Mavis with a quick-step away from The Son Of Ramses Two.

"Love that song. Absolute classic," I said, attempting to flatten my hair.

"What friggin' song? Neff, can you get this cat to stop following me."

"You know that Gloria Gaynor song. The one they always sing at gay pride parades."

"What's he want?" Mavis gestured to the cat.

I turned to see The Son Of Ramses Two looking menacingly at Mavis.

"Just a pat."

She tentatively put her hand out and then withdrew. "He's not very pat-able is he?"

"That's what Betty says."

I pulled a comb through my hair, *pink wasn't that bad, perhaps with a bit of make-up, a few clips.* "You know, Mavis, this colour is growing on me."

She said nothing.

"It's sort of bold."

"Go on, off with you!" She did a shooing motion.

The Son Of Ramses Two ignored her, circling closer.

"I never thought of pink as a bold colour. Perhaps it's time to—"

"Shoo!"

I turned to Mavis. "It's probably best if you, you know, obey him."

Mavis looked up. "What?"

"I told you. He wants a pat."

"I'm not patting him, he has the eyes of a snake."

"Don't say that, he'll hear you."

"He is a cat."

"Yes with feelings and moods swings. It's best if you humour him."

"You spoil that cat," she scolded.

"Don't say that you'll upset him."

"That is ridiculous."

"Just pat him, Mavis."

"Shoo," she said.

"I wouldn't do that."

The Son Of Ramses Two glared at her.

"Why?" Mavis glared at *me*.

The Son Of Ramses Two hissed.

He hissed again.

"Oh my god.'

"Quick, get some chicken," I said, backing off.

"What?"

"Wait." I raced to the fridge, ripped a chunk from my emergency chicken carcass and tossed it to the hissing and spitting cat.

"Chicken," I said to Mavis. "It's the only thing that works when he gets all hissy."

She stared at him. "No wonder that cat is getting fatter and fatter."

Chapter Eleven

SEX AND GEAR STICKS

There is more to a turban than a religion

Sheryl

A few days later I walked into Mum's kitchen to find Neff sporting a colourful turban, Mum circling the kitchen in her wheelchair with an empty wine bottle on her lap, and the cricket blaring from the living room.

Ms Frasier had just left and they were both celebrating.

Neff and Mum were hardly friends, they had nothing in common except, it seemed, their irritation with Ms Frasier. The mere mention of her had them spitting insults and chuckling like school boys.

According to Mum Ms Frasier had hogged the whole morning talking about some garden project that Mum had as much interest in as the sex life of her cat. Gardens were for sitting in, for cats to catch mice in, and that was about as far as it got with Mum while Ms Frasier saw a project in the making.

"She droned on like a cricket match." Mum sounded a little inebriated. "That was the only way I could get rid of her, told her George was set for watching the cricket."

George, clutching a full bottle of red, appeared in the doorway. "Thank fuck for that?"

"Fuck for what?" I said.

Mum swerved her wheelchair to face me. "There is no need to swear."

"But *he* did," I said, pointlessly. Mum after a glass of wine had the logic of a banana.

"Ms Frasier's gone," said George. "Care of herself over there." He gestured to Neff.

Neff gave a regal nod. She was sitting by the window stroking Mum's cat which was sunning on the sill. Everyone calls the cat, Puss, apart from Neff who couldn't bring herself to use the same name as her own "dear departed cat".

"Top up?" offered George.

Neff pushed her glass forward with a, "Yes, please."

George poured, then gestured to me. I told him I was driving, which went over his head as he still poured me one, telling us all how Ms Frasier was driving him crazy. "Watching cricket with her is like watching it with a visually impaired commentator who knows fuck all about cricket."

I turned to Mum expecting a reprimand, but she said nothing.

"I was at the point of chewing the couch," said George, "when Neff came in, plonked herself next to Ms Frasier and started on about "the bus ride that was so much more". God save the couch..." He toasted.

"Hear, hear," said Mum.

"...and Neff," George finished.

"Absolutely." Mum's eyes were on George like he was the Messiah, like he had just discovered the meaning of life – or at least how to half her electricity bill.

I must have looked confused because Mum began to talk to me like I was a child explaining about Neff's "moment on the bus" and how Ms Frasier doesn't do moments.

"Well, not others," said George.

Which set Mum off, giggling herself silly. At what I had no idea, until I spied the wine bottles by the bin; they had arsed three.

"Are you pissed, Mother?"

"I told you not to swear," she said.

I was about to argue, tell her that every man and his friggin' dog –

including hers – swears in her house, when George, with a chuckle, ruffled Mum's hair.

That stopped me in my tracks.

Ruffling Mum's hair is like ruffling the head of a pit bull terrier. I wouldn't do it with an iron glove but there she was giggling with the innocence of a geisha, and before I had time to work out why, Neff turned to me and said, "You're still young, you'll remember–"

"My Sheryl?" snorted Mum.

"…Just discovered sex-sex," said Neff with a cryptic look.

I stared at her. *What was she talking about?*

Neff gestured to Mum and George. "They say they don't remember. But I do."

"Put Ms Frasier right off the cricket," George said.

Mum turned to me but inclined her head towards Neff. "She had a moment, a life changing moment, an aha moment, a "so that's what it's all about vision", on the friggin' bus."

I was seriously getting fed up' going around in circles with the inebriated is hard enough when you're pissed, but sober would stir the comatose to anger. Chewing the couch was beginning to feel like an option. "I thought it was something about sex?" I said.

"I've never had one of those, you know," Mum had a serious hint of a slur, "one of those, *moments*, that is." She looked at Puss. "Have I, Puss?"

Puss answered Mum with a silent meow.

"Well, I have." George's was a definite slur. "You don't serve in the Army without a moment or two."

"You were a mechanic," Mum pointed out.

"Still saw things."

"Will you get to the point," I yelled.

Puss stood up with a prolonged back arch and yawned. No one else said anything.

Puss began to parade, her tail waving like a flag. Neff ran her hand along the cat's back with an annoying poignant look.

"Tell her about the couple on the bus," said George. "You do it so well."

"Ah, yes. The young." Neff nodded. "Their craving for passion."

"Neff, the only thing you crave is attention." I muttered. No one heard.

Neff, stood up, straightened her turban, which was perfectly straight, and began to tell me about a young couple on the bus who couldn't keep their hands off each other. All the time she paced the kitchen like it was a stage and she was in the throes of a Shakespearean monologue.

Puss watched, entranced, like Neff was about to shower her with pieces of leftover chicken, while Mum and George waited, apparently on the edge of *their* seats as if she was going to spout forth a new Sermon on the Mount. I began to wonder where I'd put the car keys.

Then she spun to face me. "Do you remember when you were young."

"I am still young."

"Sheryl," snapped Mum. "Don't be rude."

"...And your body was a mystery? New sensations every day?"

Puss let out a hopeful meow.

"Pff. Try having a baby," I muttered.

"...When lust beats through your every fibre."

Neff in the throes of lust was as hard to picture as Steven in a boxing ring. She looked about as passionate as a tombstone.

"...When you are so fired up you just have to do it and no matter where. Against a tree, in a car, a bus shelter, fuck the gear stick, fuck the wet grass, the sand, the snails, the slugs...ok not the slugs."

I looked at Mum, expecting her to tell Neff to stop, to say, "You've gone too far"."

But she was spellbound.

"...Just take me now, goddam it," screamed Neff, startling Puss into a skid and running away, disappearing like a ferret.

"You should write that down, Neff." Mum sighed.

"Hear, hear," said George.

"Write what down?" I asked.

Neff smiled at Mum. "Remember Brute?"

Mum with a shaky reverse of her wheelchair, pulled a bottle of whisky from the cupboard.

"Haven't you had enough?" I said, scarily like my mother.

"The other day I was in the Red Cross and there it was, a bottle of Brute…" said Neff.

Mum, misty-eyed, pulled out three whisky glasses.

I looked at George. "Brute?"

"Aftershave," he muttered. "Very seventies."

"I wish Steven wore aftershave," I muttered.

"…Just a whiff and I was back there. Back to that time when life was unravelling like a great big adventure." Neff sighed.

"Poetic," muttered Mum.

"Inspirational." said George.

"I'm serious, Neff, you should write that down, I'd read it," said Mum. "Better than the same old, same old…in the library."

Neff looked at her. I looked at her. *What was Mum on? Happy pills?*

"Let's not get carried away, luv," said George.

"I'm serious," Mum insisted. "Women want to read about these things, real earthy pelvis-ie things."

"I could call it "Sex and the Pelvis," said Neff.

"They do go together." I couldn't help myself; I was impressed with my wit.

"I could interview women," Neff went on. "Older women, ask them what they remember, what they miss." She turned from Mum to me and back. "What about you?"

"Me?"

"*Not* you. Sheryl. Your mum."

Mum, with her best cute smile, opened the whisky.

"Sex in a wheelchair," said Neff. "It would be a great angle."

Mum's face dropped and with a stiff look she slid the top straight back on the bottle. She never mentioned "the chair" and didn't like anyone else to do so either. I have seen her "accidentally" reverse onto the toes of those who did. It's one of the things I like about her, her refusal to be patronised. Neff has known my mum long enough to know that, she had witnessed the toe-crushing moments. But when Neff got caught up with an audience her mouth filter went out the window.

Mum turned to me like Neff was invisible. "So, Sheryl, when are you coming to sort my garden."

I looked at her. "Garden?"

"Yes. I've a few things to be planted."

I looked at George, who shrugged. "First I heard of it."

Neff, equally confused, paused. She, too, looked out onto Mum's overgrown garden. "Why don't you get a gardener," she said. "Someone young enough to look good without a shirt on, with a six pack."

"I have one," snapped Mum. "Called Sheryl."

At which point Neff, with one last look at Mum's frosty face, left.

Chapter Twelve

STEVEN

Commissioning is only as good as the commissioner

Sheryl

That night Steven was reading his book in bed as I had a sneaky peak at my toes and then jumped in beside him.

I know I'm obsessed with my toenails. If I am honest it fascinates me. It's only one toenail, well, two if you count the thick little end one, but I just can't stop looking.

Steven is fed up with it all, I could tell by the way he just looked at me, flicking pages of his book.

"Looking at them won't make any difference." he said.

"I wasn't looking," I told him.

"It takes months, probably a year." Steven turned a page.

I snuggled in, sliding my feet onto his. "Neff was in a weird mood today."

"Oh?"

"She was talking about cravings."

He flicked another page.

"And Brute aftershave."

He pulled a face.

"She even mentioned excited and wet; how she ached for a fumble." I rolled into his warm body.

Steven put his book down. "You fancy a fumble, then?" he said in a warm voice.

"And Mum didn't bat an eyelid."

"Was she on the wine?"

"Then Neff started talking about writing a book."

"Oh that," said Steven.

I sat up.

"How do you know?"

"She wants me to help. She texted me."

"That was quick."

"I think she was a bit pissed, she said she it was *aperitif* we speak tomorrow."

"For what?"

Steven shrugged. "Something about a pelvis. She says she's not sure where to start and could I get the ball rolling with a few recorded questions."

"She said all that in a text?"

Steven looked at me with his delicious soft eyes and smiled. "For authenticity."

"Neff is as authentic as a free range egg."

Steven chuckled. "How about an authentic fumble then?"

"Anyway, I can't see it happening now, she's totally pissed Mum off. God knows how long it will take Mum to forgive, let alone how much bribery. Definitely more than chocolate."

"Neff wants to write about herself," Steven said.

"Her...and her pelvis?"

Steven nodded.

I stared at the ceiling, Neff's friggin' "take me" monologue still a fresh memory.-"You're not going to do it, are you?"

"Let's see if she remembers what she said when she comes around."

I rolled onto my side. I thought of Neff, the tree, the gear stick... did I really want Steven to hear all that?

He switched off the light and cuddled into me, sliding his arms around my breasts. He pressed against my back with a firmness I knew wouldn't go away. "I love you," he whispered into my ear.

I thought of Neff ousted out of The Taj.

"I really do," said Steven.

I thought of Neff sleeping alone with all that passion, and began to feel sorry for her.

Steven cuddled closer. I could feel the warmth of his body. He stroked my back, then my neck. I almost purred; he had the hands of a magician, one rub and any stiffness melted away. He kissed my neck, ran his tongue along the curve.

How lucky was I, I thought *to have such a nice man to cuddle, who knew what I liked and was happy to give it. Perhaps I should give in,* I told myself, *it wouldn't take long...he had to get up early in the morning...*

Then I thought of Neff against that friggin' tree, the gearstick, the "take me..."

I turned to face Steven.

"I love you," he whispered again. He kissed me.

Neff telling my husband all her inner secrets? I pulled away. "I can't believe she wants to tell you about her sex life."

He huffed onto his back. "I thought we were having a moment."

"Won't it be embarrassing?"

"It's an interview, nothing more."

I sat up, switched on the light. "You write Westerns."

"She says I know what readers want, that I can spin things, that I'm a great writer."

"Of Westerns," I said.

"I *am* adaptable you know," Steven said.

"Yes, of fiction, not, well, erotic biography."

"I'm also a librarian, don't forget. I have read a lot of books. And it's not porn."

I looked at him. It's not like I was jealous or anything it's just that, well, Neff was so different at Mum's, even George all was ears. He'd forgotten all about the cricket, stood there spellbound, as if he was seeing a new Neff. If she could George put off cricket what could she put Steven off?

It was ridiculous, I knew – and yet was it?

"When does all this start?" I huffed.

"Not sure."

"And where is all this going to take place? Her house, I suppose."

"I don't know."

"Just you, her and her friggin' gear stick?"

"Gear stick?" he repeated.

"Yes, she does it in the car and in trees and doesn't give a flying fuck about gear sticks or…or…branches."

"You're not jealous, are you?"

"Pff, me? Of her? Hardly."

Steven looked at me. "You are, I can tell."

Baby Bea began to cry.

"I'm not. And it's your turn," I said.

Steven huffed out of bed. "It's Neff." He shoved his dressing gown on. "Not a porn star. You are just being ridiculous."

"I said I wasn't jealous."

"Completely ridiculous." He headed for the door. "Absolutely and utterly ridiculous." He slammed the bedroom door shut.

I switched off the light, rolled onto my side, and stared into the dark. A tear rolled down my cheek. What was wrong with me, picking a fight over nothing? Over Neff! I'd never seen her flirt with anyone, let alone Steven. In fact she usually acted like he wasn't there.

I started to doze, soon dreaming of a Victorian Sherlock Holmes style library, a cosy place with a big fire and loads of books…

Steven appears in a luxurious velvet smoking jacket, no trousers, and socks held up with braces. He takes a seat, slides a pipe between his lips and crosses his legs, revealing loose boxer underpants and the tail of a tie dangling.

He pulls out a pad with a pompous Sherlock Holmes air. "Carry on if you must, dear."

"Oh I must, darling," says Neff with a Marlene Dietrich voice.

She's lounging on a red velvet chaise lounge, dressed in a Victorian corset, complete with garters and a transparent silk robe covering little if any of her slim body. She lifts a cigarette, in a holder the length of a flag pole, to her lips and inhales. "Darling."

Steven removes his pipe. "Don't call me darling…darling"

"Oh darling, why not?"

"Because I absolutely can't think when you do."

"Oh darling, so sorry."

"No worries. Now let's go back to your school days. Did you wear a tunic?"

"Oh darling, you had to be there to see it."

"But I wasn't, was I, darling?"

...A door opened then shut. I felt the brush of a cold leg and was wide awake. I rolled over to cuddle Steven, the image of him in a smoking jacket had, for some reason, made me feel quite sexy. "All ok" I whispered.

Silence.

I cuddled harder. "Are you awake?"

He burst into a snore.

I gave him a shake.

He snored louder.

I huffed onto my back; the first time in ages I felt like a bit of how's your father and he was out for the count.

That man could fall asleep quicker than a sneeze.

Chapter Thirteen

DISCOVERY

One chocolate is never enough

Neff

Sometimes I wondered about Beatrice. I had phoned her three times, left messages − a and did she answer? Mavis said to give her time. Time for what, I had no idea, and did Mavis elaborate? She just told me not to play the innocent and gave me a lecture.

"What do you expect? You're going to be talking about your sex life, and there's Sheryl running out of oestrogen and wanting a baby."

"Sheryl wants a baby? I had no idea."

"Typical," *Her Majesty* huffed.

We were sitting outside by the hot tub at the time, rubbing ourselves dry.

The hot tub had been in my garden for quite some time. The Bag Lady and Betty won it in a raffle and considered it theirs − like my pyramid; the place I used to meditate under until Rodger left me and I took to drink and moaning instead.

Now The Bag Lady used it to hang her clothes on, mainly her socks, which I found a tad disrespectful.

Betty and The Bag Lady, hot tub addicts to the core, had been in there all afternoon and were still bubbling away, singing Gaelic songs. Betty had taught The Bag Lady Gaelic songs during lockdown. She said, "It was good for the brain, kept dementia at bay, which was as probable as Beatrice doing a handstand.

Betty, despite spending most evenings with me liked to think she helped her son and Rodger run The Argyll Hotel. Not that they called it help – they called it interfering.

During lockdown it nearly went under. The only thing that kept the business afloat were takeaways, which Betty claimed was her idea. They even used me to deliver them, which I wanted to think was a sign of bridges mended between me and Rodger, although he still grunted at me as if I was about to steal his last packet of crisps.

Betty and The Bag Lady spent lockdown Face Timing each other until the rule of six came into force and it was legal to meet outside in groups of six. Betty was around my garden quick smart.

At the time I had no idea. I had been on several deliveries and had arrived back from my last; a fish supper and a tandoori mixed grill, and the car was still reeking. I reversed into the drive, all windows open for a good airing, when Betty's infectious laughter peeled through the air, causing me to stall the car.

Then I heard The Bag Lady burst into song.

The Bag Lady singing was not something anyone wanted to hear, the sort of noise that hypnotised cats – my dear departed Puss couldn't get enough of it. In fact, this was the first time I had heard The Bag Lady sing since Puss keeled over in front of Boris Johnson on the TV. The Bag Lady claimed it was the spilt prawn cocktail sauce Puss licked from the floor. But it turned out my dear departed Puss had a dodgy heart, a ticking time bomb, apparently. According to the vet she could have dropped dead any time, and neither the prawns nor Boris Johnson had anything to do with it.

Anyway, I'd headed around the back, I had a decent amount of leftovers from The Taj, which I was looking forward to sharing, and what I saw was enough to make me drop my pakoras.

The two women were under my pyramid, smoking joints the size of didgeridoos. Betty was sitting like a yogi, while The Bag Lady, spliff between her lips, was attempting a downward dog and sending a dodgy pair of socks flying.

They'd smoked enough dope to raise Jimmy Hendrix from the dead.

Betty had discovered a stash of hash hidden in The Argyll's cleaning cupboard. She was giving the toilets a good going over when lockdown started and found it hidden behind the bleach. For months she had waited for the restriction to drop, for the chance to share her stash with her pal *and* give my dear departed Puss the send-off she deserved.

Inspired by "Yoga in Kilts" – a breathtaking book, according to Betty – they wrapped a tartan blanket around their swimsuits and were doing something spiritual, "in memory of my Puss." Guess that's what comes from spending your nights looking at picture books of topless men in kilts pulling yoga poises in the glens of Scotland...A pastime I thought those two ladies were well past.

Before I had a chance to rescue The Bag Lady's socks, the two of them were taking selfies like teenagers, and keeling over with laughter. It didn't take them long to work up a hunger and they were soon raiding my kitchen like dieters on a binge. They ate like they hadn't eaten for a decade, and after a packet of Digestives smothered in anything gooey, a packet of marshmallows melted on the bonfire, and the entire carry-out I had brought back with me, they fell asleep; only waking when Mavis came around to ask what the hell had been posted on my Instagram account.

Now I can't look out the window without seeing those two together, either in the hot tub, getting out of the hot tub, or sitting by the hot tub. There is not a day goes by when Betty is not there; for all I know she probably sleeps in the teepee. I smiled at the thought, wondering if there was any of the stashed hash left – when Mavis caught my eye.

Mavis had been told the stashed hash story so many times she knew it inside out. At first she laughed, but a year and many reminisces later, she took to sniffing with a stiff look, like she was fed up being reminded of a good time missed; the same sniff and stiff reaction as to my book idea. But then Mavis never understood the need to enlighten the human race, and her moods are as complex as Sheryl's have become.

I blamed The Change for that and told Sheryl to try HRT. She told me to get stuffed. Stephen said she'll come around, she just needed time to adjust to the idea of him writing about me – which I found confusing. I hadn't told Sheryl yet. I hadn't told anyone but him and Mavis, and despite Mavis calling me self-indulgent, I was still looking forward to the experience.

"Why don't you try someone else for your book?" asked Mavis, now dry and wrapped up in a blanket.

Betty peered over the bubbles of the tub. "What book?"

"Neff is writing about sex and the pelvis," The Bag Lady told her.

I frowned. "How do you know?"

"Don't they go together?" said Betty. "Sex and the pelvis?"

"It's more than sex," I said. "My book is about women, the many ages of women… the real story."

"That's not what Sheryl thinks" said The Bag Lady, which stopped me in my tracks.

"Perhaps that's why she was funny with you," Mavis said, which had me even more confused.

"I am happy to help, talk about my life," said Betty.

"Well, I'm not." The Bag Lady jumped out of the hot tub like a teenager.

I told them about my plans; that I was thinking of interviewing minority women: disabled, victims, that sort of thing. They looked at me like I was spitting nails. "You know, women who need a voice,' I explained.

"Beatrice hardly needs a voice, she's a foghorn," said The Bag Lady. "She speaks for herself before she's asked."

"But she *is* disabled," I said.

The three women glared at me like I'd grown a penis for a nose.

"That wheelchair is a weapon in her hands," said Betty. "She's run over more toes than a supermarket trolley. She's not a victim, she's a sadist."

"The wheelchair is a sellable angle," I told them. "If only I could find a lesbian. Or someone from the Far East. With different… er…skin."

"Why don't you get George, black up, put on a dress, and talk about fisting," said The Bag Lady.

That stopped us all in our tracks.

"What about Shifty and Rodger," said Betty, a comment I chose to ignore.

"You'd make a fortune," The Bag Lady continued. "The next J K Rowling."

"I don't think there are any wheelchairs in Harry Potter," I said but The Bag Lady didn't listen, she was on a roll. She ranted on about porno Harry Potter making millions and how she and Betty could have all the spliffs they wanted, top class gear, sending Mavis and Betty into a fit of the giggles.

"I just think a story from someone in a wheelchair would be a good angle," I said.

The Bag Lady, mid leg-drying, looked as convinced as a policeman with a staggering drunk saying he was sober.

"I really want to win Beatrice over..."

'Aye, right.' Mavis laughed.

"...so I thought with Steven's help I could write something about me that would impress Beatrice, let her see the spirit behind my work."

Betty switched off the hot tub, climbed out, wrapped a towel around her waist and plonked herself beside me. "That, my dear, is as believable as Beatrice being a victim."

As the hot tub shut down, the full moon peered from a cloud illuminating the hot tub. The steam subsided. The Son Of Ramses Two emerged like an apparition, poised like a statue on the corner of the hot tub. He blinked. It was an entrance he had perfected from the day he appeared.

"Has that cat put on weight?" said Betty.

The Bag Lady stopped drying herself and peered at him.

"Don't touch him," warned Mavis.

The Bag Lady ran her hands down the smooth grey fur, stopping at his stomach. The Son Of Ramses Two purred.

"Jesus," whispered Mavis. "How did you do that?"

"This cat is pregnant," The Bag Lady announced.

"Impossible," I said.

"Have you looked at its equipment?" asked Betty.

"Look at its equipment – are you kidding?" Mavis gasped.

The Son Of Ramses Two was looking up at The Bag Lady with admiration. The Bag Lady lifted him onto her knee. The Son Of Ramses Two purred louder.

Mavis gasped again. "Shall I get the chicken?"

The Bag Lady flipped the cat over and inspected his belly. The Son Of Ramses Two flopped like a rag doll, giving in to the indignity of an inspection with nothing but another purr. "What we have here," The Bag Lady confirmed, "is The *Daughter* of Ramses Two."

The Bag Lady rolled her back onto her stomach allowing The Daughter of Ramses Two to look at me with an "I did try to tell you" face. She ruffled herself sleek, then curled into The Bag Lady's lap.

"And she is definitely pregnant."

"Pregnant? Who's pregnant?" ~~Said~~ Sheryl appeared from the driveway.

Chapter Fourteen

MAKING UP

There is only so much oestrogen talk a man can take.

Sheryl

It was Steven's idea I should "visit, chill and chat", to make up for the "Get stuffed" snap, which according to him Neff didn't deserve.

At the time I thought it was a great idea. Making up in the dark, after a few drinks, is far easier than doing it sober during the day, especially with The Bag Lady and Mavis around; they're always happy to gang up on Neff. I was almost looking forward to it, until I sat in the car.

"You ready then?" Steven said.

How kind I thought, *him thinking of me and my happiness.* I slid on my jacket, slowly, while Steven stood by the front door, Baby Bea on his shoulders gently patting his head. She looked at me and laughed. *How sweet.*

Steven had offered to drive me to Neff's house so I could have a few drinks with the girls, he even offered to get up with Baby Bea during the night and in the morning as it was the weekend. I was grateful, but as we grew closer to Neff's house I started to feel angry. I don't know why. It's not like Steven said anything, he didn't say a word all the way there. Although I did catch him humming.

I had spent the day reading up on the menopause.

From the "Magic Of Menopause" to "Don't Forget The HRT", I had demolished, read and re-read every book, leaflet and blog I could get my hands – or rather, eyes – on. And it was all there: lack of periods (which I had put down to breastfeeding), head fog, hot flushes, night sweats. I couldn't sleep worrying about it all, then I read insomnia was one of the symptoms...

Why hadn't I seen it before?

When I was pregnant, Steven had raided the library for anything to do with the subject. We digested it all, back then, however the menopause was not the same, and after a couple of chapters of "Getting To Know My Uterus," he wained.

"It's all bit too oestrogen-ie for me," he muttered, with a crisp shut of the book.

Baby Bea was on my lap tucking into a flapjack at the time, and I was flipping through "The Menopause Manifesto." Steven kissed her forehead, then patted my shoulder.

I looked up. "Some call it an illness."

"You don't look ill to me."

"That's what they say about depression, don't they? You don't look ill."

He stopped. "You're not depressed, are you?"

"No, but it can happen during the menopause." I flicked a page.

Steven lifted Baby Bea, and she pushed her fingers into his mouth. He brushed them away with a kiss.

She was currently going through a happy phase, which had preceded her stomach bug phase (six months of catching every bug going), a scared of the dark phase, the much talked about playing with your food phase, which, to be honest, she was still going through, and the dreaded crying when I leave phase...Me, leaving in the morning while Steven jiggled her at the door with a desperate, "Wave goodbye to mummy," as she, screaming, pushed his hands away in temper. It was a phase I hated, but strangely missed once she stopped.

There were other phases, which had been studied by Steven, like he was swotting for an exam. The "hitting sleeping Dad on the couch for fun" phase – a phase videoed and up on Instagram, (I wasn't sure if Steven had seen that yet). Baby Bea's cartoons put Steven to sleep quicker than a fumble, and it was that which led to a "let's see what wakes Dad experiments" from Baby Bee: lip pulling, prodding and licking, eye poking, and her famous it-always-works scrunching Dad's face with a nose lick...Until she discovered Sesame Street. The programme kept her so entertained, even I joined in on a couch snooze when it was on.

The "tossing teddy out of the cot in a tantrum" phase, only happened after Steven or I snuggled teddy into the cot to make her sleep. A useless ploy which led to frustration on both sides, more tossing, less snuggling on the part of me and Steven, and more hurling rather than throwing on Baby Bea's part. Teddy tossing was a desperate measure; four o'clock in the morning tantrums can do that to a parent. Steven, came up with tossing teddy in the air for a laugh. Baby Bea laughed so much she couldn't resist doing it herself and spent hours in her cot juggling teddy into the air and giggling, until teddy landed on the floor.

Babies, it seemed, were as complicated to get to grips with as underneath the bonnet of a car, and Steven coped with books. His eBook Reader was crammed with parenting books. He had more eBooks than Amazon. From, "The Crib Sheet" to "Be Your Baby's Best friend", he read them all, and when they didn't work he sat Baby Bea near the kitchen bench in her high chair and baked cakes. Letting her lick the spoon soothed many tantrums – almost as many as stroking Puss, Beatrice's cat.

"You should write a manual," I often joked.

Until Neff's stupid idea came along.

Steven leant across me and opened the car door. I fanned a smile.

"Go on," he said. "Have a good time, you know you always do."

I looked at him. Did he mean that?

Steven waited for me to get out of the car – a little too happy for my liking.

You just want rid of me, don't you? I thought. My stomach tightened. I turned to see Baby Bea gleefully waving a carrot stick at me, something only friggin' Steven could get her to eat.

"Enjoy yourself and come back refreshed, luv," he said.

Refreshed – just another word for pissed and rearing for a fumble.

I started to feel angry, like the whole world was against me. Steven wasn't thinking about my happiness at all he was thinking about a drunken me gagging for it. He'd fumble every night if he could, it always put him to sleep while I lay there shaken like a Martini, staring at the ceiling, sleep as possible as, well, me getting pregnant. I was just a sleeping friggin' pill to him.

God, this was exhausting, like being pregnant again. My moods swinging like a thurible in a church, as up down as my libido, which apparently is what happens during the menopause. That and getting a midriff. And did Steven care, did he fuck, he didn't give a shit.

"Paranoia is a great storyteller," he kept saying, until I pointed out it wasn't paranoia but a lack of oestrogen.

I stomped out of the car, clutching my bag of something not red, something that didn't stain my teeth, didn't make my stomach queasy, didn't give me a hangover.

Another sign of The friggin' Change.

"Have fun," he said, giving me a weird look, then drove off. Baby Bea was in the back, using her carrot stick like a royal flag.

"Bye, darling," I muttered after them.

She didn't even look back.

The fire was already blazing when I appeared. The Bag Lady had that cat on her knee, while the others looked up, laughing, with an "oh, you're here" look.

"Sheryl's here, stop talking about her," shouted Mavis, which was as funny as the first time I heard a decade ago.

In fact, "Very funny," was on the tip of my tongue – swear word undecided – when I caught sight of Neff, sporting a lopsided turban with way too much pink hair peeking out to be intentional. Neff always wore her long black tresses dark, trussed up in ethnic scarves, turbans and head bands. Black being, as she claimed, her natural colour. The pink stopped me in my tracks. Mavis was right, that hairdresser had as much idea of hair colour as a blind painter and decorator.

Neff, seeing me looking, straightened her turban with a sheepish look, and my anger melted.

Steven had said tonight was The Bag Lady's idea to celebrate the long dark winter nights with a bonfire. Not that she needed an excuse, or even a rain-free day, she'd sit under an umbrella for a bonfire if she could. Turns out, though, this was all a set-up, a plot for Neff and me to make up under the stars. My head was too busy; I'd had no idea till much later.

Chapter Fifteen

GO BOY

Nights out are not the same when you're feeding a wee one

Sheryl

Betty and Mavis were at the entrance to The Bag Lady's teepee, Betty intermittently singing a Gaelic song, which Mavis was attempting to join in – not the easiest thing to do after way too many wines.

Hot and flushed, I squeezed in next to Mavis, making sure I was as far away as possible from that cat of Neff's. I nearly fell off when I saw him splayed across The Bag Lady's lap like an upside down rag doll.

I was speechless. That cat would have your arm off if you looked at him the wrong way. He was always appearing from nowhere, sleek, thin, and statue-still, daring you to look twice. Intimidating as a policeman with a breathalyser, the cat had as much ability to look comfortable as a stiletto. Yet there he was, sprawled out like a fallen drunk who couldn't be arsed getting up, as round as a Russian doll, as threatening as a block of chocolate and looking as comfortable as I felt in an old bra.

I really hated that cat.

"He's put on weight," I said, which sent the women into a frenzy of laughter.

Neff poured me a drink and I was just about to sip it, when The so-called Son Of Ramses Two rolled onto his feet and *made for my lap.* I stopped, glass poised. "What's he doing?" He climbed onto my lap. I froze. "He's never done this before."

Neff laughed.

I attempted a tentative pat. "What's he want? Why me?"

"*He* is a *she*," said Neff.

"You're joking!" I spluttered. That cat was as feminine as a wrestler in drag.

I looked down at the smooth head of Neff's cat, now sprinkled with a few drops of my wine. I watched him...her position herself in her usual don't-touch-me seated pose. I attempted another stroke, expecting the glare of a lifetime. Instead, she eyed me with a silent meow.

"Funny cat, isn't he...er...I mean, she," I said.

"She doesn't like it if you're timid." The Bag Lady grabbed The Daughter of Ramses Two with a sort of roughness that had me gasping, then rolled her onto her back and ruffled her belly. The Daughter of Ramses Two purred. I marvelled at The Bag Lady.

"You just need to show her who's the boss." The Daughter of Ramses Two looked up at her with admiration, The Bag Lady ruffled the cat's head, "We're a complete narcissist, aren't we?"

I swear I saw the cat nod.

"She's royalty," snapped Neff, straightening her turban for the hundredth time since I arrived, "and we need to find a better name, The Daughter of Ramses Two just doesn't have the same ring to it."

"Perhaps you could skip the Two?" said Mavis.

"She's royal," shouted Neff.

"What's that got to do with it?" Mavis shouted back.

"All royals have numbers after their names." Neff headed for her kitchen.

The Daughter of Ramses Two blinked at me warmly. She tilted her head at me and blinked again...all cosy like.

"There something wrong with this cat," I said. "I swear she smiled at me."

Betty let out a drunken cackle, sparking off Go Boy next door. The

Daughter of Ramses Two jumped from my knee, her claws oblivious to my flesh.

I screeched.

"Simmer down," yelled Jason's voice.

Bark! Bark!

"That'll do" Jason bellowed.

Neff appeared at her back door, tying up a full-to-the-brim rubbish bag. She re-opened it and attempted a squashing down manoeuvre with her foot, a shoving with her hand, then repeated the foot stamping. She was just about to attempt further squashing with the lid when The Daughter of Ramses Two bounded past.

She skidded across the top of the bin, her claws catching the plastic.

Rip.

Bark.

A few chicken bones tumbled to the ground.

The Daughter of Ramses Two followed them. With an undignified scramble, she skidded, stumbled to her paws, and shot past Neff like a bolt of black lighting, almost knocking her for six.

"What's up with her?" I said.

The others laughed.

"Go Boy," muttered Neff, picking up the bin lid. She stood up with a sigh.

The Daughter of Ramses Two appeared on the kitchen window sill looking weirdly scared.

Bark! Bark!

"Shut it or you get this over your fucking head," shouted Jason's voice.

The Daughter of Ramses Two disappeared, reappeared, and hurled herself at Neff. Neff stumbled, staggered and tripped over the bin.

Bark! Bark!

Whack.

Neff righted herself, and The Daughter of Ramses Two clambered up to sit on her shoulders, digging her claws into Neff's turban.

Whack.

Yelp.

"Get inside now," thundered Jason.

Neff's turban began to slide to the side. The Daughter of Ramses Two, with an "oh shit" look, clung like a log in the middle of the sea.

The turban began to unravel.

The Daughter of Ramses Two followed, cascading down Neff's back with desperate scrabbling. I actual felt sorry for her. She landed on the ground with an undignified plop – followed by the ex-turban pile of silk.

Neff's bright pink hair bun sprung upright from the crown of her head, and The Daughter of Ramses Two, attempting a "regaining dignity" paw lick, caught sight of Neff's hair and stopped dead.

"Jesus," muttered Betty, from behind Mavis, and clutching the biggest cocktail I had ever seen.

A few hours later Mavis was combing Neff's hair, tugging it free from a construction of pins as complicated as a Rubik's cube.

"How many pins did you use?" she said, slipping another into her lap.

I don't think the alcohol was helping.

I watched with affection, without a hint of jealousy or anger. Those feelings had disappeared the moment I spied the luminous bun perched on the top of Neff's head like a pink light bulb. It was the worst hair style I had ever seen, not even the aloofness of The Daughter of Ramses Two could pull off that stupid look.

"Did you hide your hair even from the cat?" I blurted out.

Neff blushed. "Of course not." She attempted a casual stroll to a seat, The Daughter of Ramses Two circling her, eyes on the pink hair.

"For you." Said Betty, offering me a large glass of something.

"It's a smoothie." Mavis winked. "With an added something for a kick."

I looked at the scarily healthy-looking drink.

"Where's yours?" I said.

"We ran out of tofu" said Mavis.

"It has tofu in it?" asked The Bag Lady.

"Sorry, soya, not tofu," Mavis corrected herself.

"Same friggin' thing," muttered The Bag Lady.

"Soya?" I said, mid sip. "On a night out?"

"Apparently it's good for The Change," said Betty.

The Bag Lady rolled her eyes. "That's as believable as Neff's pink hair." She looked at me. "Let me pour you a wine."

I shook my head. Mavis and Betty's smoothie/cocktail was delicious. Apparently it was brimming with "nature's oestrogen". An impressive looking drink, it came in a cocktail glass, with an erect banana, a cocktail umbrella, an eco-friendly straw and a cocktail sparkler. It was the sort of drink that that deserved a ta-dah and lots of oohs and ahhs rather than the up-staging of Neff's hair.

"Not like in my day," Betty was going on. "Back then it was HRT and antidepressants – drugs all the way."

"That explains a lot," said The Bag Lady.

Mavis sipped her wine. "The Japanese eat soya and they don't even have a word for hot flushes."

"That's what Steven says," I muttered.

"What would he know?" The Bag Lady scoffed.

"He reads a lot." Betty put on her "I am expert" look.

"I passed all that without a hiccup," said Neff. "Care of hip circles and pelvic tilts."

"Yams," suggested Betty. "Some say yams are good."

"Tenzam says they use things like that," Neff agreed.

"I thought yams came from Africa?" said Betty.

"Oh. Maybe it was jackfruit, then," muttered Neff. She sipped her wine. "Sorry, not jackfruit, fenugreek."

"What's that when it at home?" Mavis asked.

"It's for indigestion," said The Bag Lady.

"As well as menopause," said Neff. "It's a miracle spice. What those Asians don't know about spice is not worth knowing. Spices are the fountain of youth." She shook her hair.

"We'll need to sort that hair of yours," said Mavis, caught in the crossfire. "Let me dye it purple for you. And paint your toenails to match."

The Daughter of Ramses Two interrupted Neff's answer by jumping on my knee again, this time curling up *and* falling asleep.

"What the hell is wrong with this cat?" I said. Again.

"She's pregnant," said The Bag Lady.

"Oh," I muttered. "Lucky her." I ran my hand along her back, feeling sternly calm. I guess that's what comes of stroking a pregnant cat that no longer wants to bite.

She purred.

"I really wanted another child," I said.

"Maybe you still can," said Mavis, "I know of women who–"

"I went through The Change in my twenties," interrupted The Bag Lady.

No one said anything.

"Never had the chance for a baby," she carried on, her expression flat.

The fire flickered in the silence as we all waited for more. The Bag Lady usually gave away nothing, and over the years I had stopped guessing about her past – if there was a partner, or a child. Sometimes I even wondered if she came into this world old and homeless. Now, as she stared into the almost-out fire, I wanted to know everything. I was as curious as Agatha Christie's Poirot.

Silence.

I looked from Mavis to Betty. Betty shrugged.

'Tell me more," I was about to scream – when Neff jumped in, her hair free and wild, blowing in the evening breeze like a pink haystack.

"I have found The New Me," she announced. Dramatically.

"Well's that obvious." Mavis laughed.

Who cares I thought.

"...Something better. Something creative..."

"You mean, your book," I said.

"...My book about Women." She turned to The Bag Lady.

The Bag Lady looked up.

"Like your story," said Neff. "I would love to write your story."

Chapter Sixteen

MEMOIRS

Everything you wanted to know about a belly dancer and were too afraid to ask?

Sheryl

Steven had his first session with Neff in our living room, when Baby Bea was at nursery and I was working.

I arrived home after work to find Baby Bea still in her highchair, waving a fist full of mashed toast and Steven loading the dishwasher with a queer look on his face.

"Did it not go well?" I asked.

"I am at the "rights of her…er…passages," he said.

I laughed.

He shut the dishwasher. "And they are long and winding."

Baby Bea tossed the decapitated crust onto the ground.

Steven bent to retrieve it and wipe the floor. "Some bits *are* funny, some even poignant." He tossed the crust at the bin with a spectacular miss. "But there is so friggin' much of it, I can't find a pivotal point."

Steven was very fond of his pivotal points. He was always going on about them, and if he couldn't find one, it fair put him off his toasted cheese – the very thing he craves when lost in a story.

I watched him move to wipe Baby Bea's hands. She got to his face first, patting the remains of jam and mashed toast onto his cheeks.

"It will take me ages to type it all up, let alone make it into a story."

Steven cleaned Baby Bea's hands and face then lifted her from the highchair. She raced to me for a hug. He washed his face.

"I had no idea how much work..." He sighed, and with a long look at me and Baby Bea muttered, "I better get started."

Baby Bea and I watched as he picked up his phone and made for his "writing space".

When working in the library Steven scribbles notes in his notebook; in fact, there are notebooks scattered everywhere, from his side of the bed, to the car, the kitchen, even the toilet, all of which find their way, alongside his phone recordings, to his writing space under our stairs. He tried the spare room, then the shed, then the kitchen but in the end, squeezing himself under the stairs was what worked best. Well, that a ton of black coffee and some decent Cheddar. According to Steven being boxed in helped him focus, stimulating his creative juices.

It was the lack of outlook, apparently. "The only thing I can look at is the computer screen, and that calendar of yours."

Of course it helped to have the ability to switch off, which he does – like the computer. Once he pulled the dressing screen around him he was in another world, oblivious to Baby Bea and I skirting about the tiny space left in the hallway. Nothing disturbed him, even when Baby Bee peeked her head around the screen – usually to shove a half-eaten biscuit in Steven's face.

He paused at the kitchen door. "I'm going in..."

"Do you want me to make some toasted cheese?"

"Not now," he said with a wave of his hand. He made to close the door (the last thing the writing place is, is soundproof) then peeked around.. "But let me know when you're heading off to bed." The door shut behind him.

I heard the scrape of the screen, then Steven stir his coffee in that thinking way of his. An excessive, way over the top stir, considering his coffee black was with no sugar. And it went on forever, as if he was contemplating the saving of a planet or rewriting the laws of gravity, mixing friggin cement and was usually followed with a loud long sip, by which time I'd be crawling the ceiling wanting to scream, "Just drink the stuff."

Finally he sipped and Neff's voice started.

"The passages of my life are like the passages of dance routines... Oh no, sorry, don't use that...The true calling of a shimmy is not for the faint-hearted...Bollocks, don't use that either...Hell, where do I start?"

"How about with your childhood?" said Steven's voice.

Chapter Seventeen

TAPE RECORDINGS

There are many sides to a cat's meow

Sheryl

Neff rarely talked of her "pre Lochgilphead" days – apart from her ex, Rodger, and even that was patchy. All most people knew about was her famed arrival, riding into Lochgilphead on a brightly-coloured moped, wearing matching leathers.

She stopped traffic back then.

It has been years since she scooted about on her moped in that pink leather. She sold both after she was stopped by the police for driving too slowly on the motorway. Now she drives a car.

Neff is a long lean woman who likes bright, ethnic outfits. She dresses like something out of a second-hand African shop, but no-one ever batted an eyelid. Even when they walked into The Taj to find her sporting a six inch high turban and packing pakoras to belly dancing music. She'd been there so long her look was as predictable as the local bus, and her ways no weirder than a roll and sausage. Even I had become used to her, but when she started to talk of a childhood I had no idea about, I just had to listen. Neff as a child was hard enough to imagine...but her parents? What the hell were they like?

Baby Bea was waiting for our usual clearing up routine, normally performed to music. Steven had filled the dishwasher, so it was a mere sweeping of his bin misses and anything else flung by Baby Bea, while she waved the dust brush around like it was a magic wand. I decided on something quiet and pulled out Baby Bea's playdough.

There was something soothing about playdough on the floor with a toddler, especially when you were earwigging in on someone else's conversation. But Baby Bea had no intention of rolling it. She picked up a lump of playdough and began to squish and squash with relish, watching it ooze through her fingers like she had never seen it before.

She giggled until we heard Neff speak again: "We were poor, I can tell you," then stopped and gazed around as if she were expecting Neff to walk in. When she didn't, Baby Bea resumed her squishing.

"Bread and butter was a luxury, fruit as accessible as a fur coat. There was more food in a back packer's lunch than our cupboards." Neff's voice rang out, and Steven started to stir *again*. "Sometimes I'd open the cupboard to a packet of Quaker oats standing like a loan soldier in the mist of a glen." She was always dramatic. "Porridge; I hate the frigging stuff. Mum would pour it into a drawer to set, then slice it up for me to take to school. I was so hungry I ate it before I arrived...I walked miles to school, in shoes with more holes than a sieve. Whenever it rained my socks were soaking. Until, that is, an uncle appeared..."

Steven stopped stirring.

"...He was walking around our flat like he owned the place. The first uncle was like a prince from the Far East. He'd arrive with an arm full of parcels, drop them at my feet, then pick up my mum and swirl her about until they kissed. It was like living in a Disneyland film when he was there." I could hear the smile in Neff's voice. "My mum sang to herself, the cupboards were groaning with food, and I was skipping to school with dry socks and sandwiches stuffed with butter and cheese." There was a pause then, "He had a strong thick accent, smoked foreign cigarettes and smelt exotic, which I now realise was garlic. He taught Mum to cook food I had never tasted before; even now when I look at an aubergine I get all misty-eyed." Neff let out one of her dramatic sighs.

Baby Bea began to smash her playdough like she was killing it. "Ya Ya YA!"

"Shh."

"...He used to circle his hips to Jimmy Shand, and I'd count..."

"I thought you lived in Norwich," said Steven.

"We did but Mum had a Scottish accent, which the prince from the East absolutely loved. He gave Mum flowers and filled our bathroom with perfumes and aftershave, the sort you never saw in Boots." Another sigh. "The first time he disappeared, Mum was quiet, and I was crying, I thought he'd died. Then we seemed to get used to the disappearing, the waiting at the door, realising "not tonight." He'd disappear for weeks, months, then appear like Santa Claus, drop parcels at my feet, pick up Mum and swirl her about till she laughed. The last time I saw him I was ten. He dropped me off at school and everyone stared at his dark skin." Neff's voice dropped. "There were few other uncles after that – but none like him."

"When you say a few," said Steven, "how many do you mean?"

"One or two..." Neff paused. "Three or four. One made to slap me, but Mum shoved him out the door and I never saw that one again." When she continued, she sounded reflective. "I like to think that perhaps the prince from the East was my father, but I have no idea. I don't look like him. I don't even look like my mother. I am the spitting image of my grandfather. Ironic really, as the only time I saw *him*, he was actually spitting. He was in the sort of care home that stank of pee...He had a hunted look, growled like a bear when anyone came near and it took several men to hold him down to give him an injection. Mum left crying, until the uncle that slapped me appeared. I remember, it was the very same night he tried to slap me. She was ferocious."

"Did your uncle, the 'prince' teach you to belly dance?" Steven asked.

Neff laughed. "It would be a nice story if it were true. No, he did teach my mum how to make a curry though. I learnt to belly dance years later when I was working in the ex's cafe."

"Rodger had a cafe?" I was as surprised as Steven sounded.

"No. My first husband."

"You had a husband?" I was even more surprised than Steven sounded.

"I married at eighteen. A big handsome man. He worked for a builder, who was doing up the flat above us. He appeared at the door one day, clutching an empty kettle, looking for water. Mum ended up making coffee for all the workers. She'd bring up a tray every day and he – the ex – brought it down again..." After a minute, Neff went on, "He was the sort of man who could persuade anyone to do anything. He had a smile, a look that softened folk. He didn't have to take or steal, he just threw a few admiring looks, a few charming words, and people gave him things. Like the café. It was given to him by an aunt. "Do it up and it's yours," she told him."

"And he did."

"Yes. Doing that old thing up cost him next to nothing, he wangled favours like a politician. Before I knew it I was married, working my socks off in the kitchen, while he was in the front seducing customers to bring in their families and friends. Mind, it all changed..."

"When?" Steven prompted her.

'When he couldn't have children. It was like he blamed me..."

I stopped concentrating solely on Neff and looked at Baby Bea.

"...Like I was there to do a job and when I didn't, I didn't exist. Soon I was sleeping on my own, and cooking meals he didn't eat. He was hardly there. In fact the only time I saw him was at the café, where he "entertained". By the time I realised he'd dipped his penis into more fannies than I'd made cappuccinos my mum was dying and I was feeling pretty sorry for myself. Until..." Neff's voice dipped then brightened slightly. "Until a group of women came in from a local belly dancing class. They looked so happy – just like my exotic uncle.

"I was known as Janice back then. I stood in the back of the class and said little, sometimes wondering what I was doing there. One day the ex saw me dance and laughed...Don't know why I was so angry. But it really got my goat and I was determined to prove him wrong."

At tha moment, Baby Bea started to rub her eyes. I lifted her and took her to her room for her bedtime feed.

Chapter Eighteen

MORE MEMOIRS

How we see ourselves is often a surprise to others

Sheryl

By the time Baby Bea was drinking, half-sleep, Neff was still being dramatic, and I was all ears.

"There is nothing more frightening than starting again, especially with nothing," she was saying. 'And I had less than nothing. I was so scared I couldn't eat; I didn't think I could take care of myself. I was so used to being in the wrong I just assumed, well, I was an idiot. I had been invisible for years."

I stroked Baby Bee's cheek. *As if, Neff had the ego of a diva.*

"My mother had died and the ex was all I had. Walking out on him meant walking into No Man's Land with empty pockets. Apparently, the cafe made as much money as a paper round – on its last legs. He blamed me, of course, said I was too up myself." Neff snorted. "As if. He was the one up himself. He couldn't pass a female, no matter what age, without a bit of flirting. And quite frankly, I was sick of it."

A memory came back to me then: of Neff by the fire, talking of chipped stilettos and blow jobs and how no man could resist either. She wasn't drunk or anything, she was sober and trying to reassure Betty, who was feeling pretty low at the time. I'd never heard Neff use the term *blow job* before, but that night she threw it around like she was emptying a cold mug of coffee.

"...I walked in on her and him," said Neff. "That chipped stiletto... Well, the first thing I saw was her red heels in the air. Then her legs. Then I heard him grunt, saw his dimpled arse..."

She paused.

I heard Steven sip his coffee.

"You don't have to tell me everything," he said, on the tape.

"...in the sort of position, a dog would be ashamed of..."

She paused.

He sipped.

"...It looked humanly impossible..."

"As I said you don't have to tell me." Steven's voice sounded strained.

"On a table..."

She never mentioned a table that other night.

"...Cream teas *s*cattered to the winds."

"I get the picture," muttered Steven.

"She was older than me. Legs as dimpled as orange peel, and *not* the sort you expect to see wearing stiletto heels."

"More coffee," Steven said loudly.

"She had the libido of a rabbit" said Neff.

"Sugar?"

"Between you and me I did know about her but seeing it...nothing prepares you for that." Her voice lowered. "He hadn't touched me in years. And there, *there* he was without a care for the tablecloth, or the scones and jam smashed to a pile of crumbs unfit for even a sparrow. I went off tablecloths after that. And cream teas."

I'm not surprised, I thought.

"I can't look at a scones without see his grunting backside."

"You've put me off scones, and all." Said Steven.

"You only have to see one smashed under a pulsating thigh–"

"Yes! I can imagine."

"She was stinking rich, too. She saved his business."

"I see," muttered Steven.

"As well as the sort who could do porno blow jobs any man would die for..."

Steven had a coughing fit.

"...How could I compete? Not that I wanted to."

Silence.

Then I heard Steven push the dressing screen open.

It never took long for my bedtime feed to put her to sleep. A few minutes on one breast and her eyes were closed and her head slumped to the side, like she was stoned. I lifted her to her cot. For a second her eyes opened, she smiled at me then flopped back to sleep. Breast milk always did that to her.

I thought about Neff; all that passion and disappointment and still she wore pink. Still she believed, still she carried on...I groaned. *Why* had I told her to get stuffed?

I thought of the night by the bonfire and her ruined hair, and had this huge urge to make it better, to charge over there and dye her hair a better colour, to tell her something nice, even give her hug. Not that she'd want one; she's not that sort.

Steven appeared by my side, wrapped his arm around my waist, and peered into the cot.

"Nit, nit Bea," he whispered.

Chapter Nineteen

THE SCRAP BOOK

A kind heart can often come from the least expected place

Neff

When Sheryl joined our bonfire my heart sank, I had no idea she was coming and I wasn't in the mood for, well, *her* mood.

I had enough to deal with – my hair, for a start. How anyone would take me seriously with my shit pink hair was beyond me, and Mavis being ridiculously hopeful didn't help. I had almost convinced myself that it was ok, until The Daughter of Ramses Two froze like she had seen a headless chicken tap-dancing. Gloria Gaynor's "I am what I am" mantra went out the window quicker than a belch. If the cat was dumbstruck what the hell would others think?

Mavis threw me one of her looks and I threw one back.

"You and Sheryl need to make peace," she whispered more than once. As if she was a beacon of success. Like her life was bulging with friends.

I was very surprised when The Bag Lady handed Sheryl her notebook to read.

I'd thought she might tell us more about her life. I mean, throwing out the "I couldn't have children" bombshell and then just sitting back like that, how could she? We were all waiting, wondering what would come next, then she disappeared into her teepee and reappeared with her scrapbook.

The same scrapbook she had given to me all those years ago, the one that had helped me through the tough times of Rodger and Shifty.

Not many knew of The Bag Lady's scrapbook, apart from Betty... and, well...Mavis, which probably meant Lumpy knew as well. Mavis did assure me she had "kept shtum", something I found hard to believe. Mavis, after a few gins, wines or whatever, leaked gossip like a sieve. Lumpy, thank heavens, was a different story he, like Betty, had the sealed lips of a stuck jam jar. And I liked it that way.

It wasn't like the bible or anything – the scrapbook, I mean – but there was something about it that cheered the soul. I found it a great comfort when Rodger left me, especially when I wrote my "Beryl Story" in it, as The Bag Lady had suggested. In fact, I had thought the scrapbook was mine to keep, to have in my home forever, so I opened my heart, my soul, in that book.

The Beryl Story was not just a story to me, it was the beginning of my new life; how I became Nefertiti the belly dancer; how I found the balls to move on. There was nothing mystical about it, or about Beryl, for that matter. It was a story as ordinary as a Co-op bag and just for me, The Bag Lady at a push, Betty and Mavis grudgingly, but definitely not Sheryl or Steven. One glass of whisky and they'd be telling Beatrice, who'd tell George, who'd tell his sister, who'd would tell the whole friggin' town. That woman could reach an audience wider than the local paper and that's before she posted on Facebook.

I would become as normal as a face cloth, the mystic of Nefertiti lost forever like dishwater down the drain. Not that these bozos camping out in my garden understood. The Bag Lady and Betty, with as much respect as an atheist in a cathedral, had taken the scrapbook from my home to "update" – two women who argued over everything.

And update with what? Bonfire recipes?

Betty said she had stories to tell, a past worth sharing – hardly an excuse, and I was about to shout that out again tonight, until I caught sight of Sheryl's face. She looked excited, like she was flicking through the pages of a James Patterson pre-order. Then when The Bag Lady told her to take it home to read, her face lit right up.

"Steven is welcome to read as well," she said.

That had me spitting chips.

After Sheryl left with *my* book under *her* arm, I told The Bag Lady that the last thing I needed was the whole town knowing the very innards of my brain.

She replied that, "The innards of your brain are hardly in that scrapbook and a wee story about some so-called psychic called Beryl won't even light a candle, let alone set Lochgilphead ablaze."

"How very friggin' insulting," I said, which had Betty topping up their glasses with an annoying chuckle.

I threw a wobbly, a complete and utter tantrum. "Being a belly dancer is illusive, mystical," I yelled, sparking a fit of barking from Go Boy.

The Bag Lady and Betty said nothing.

"I'm going to get it back," I screamed.

The Bag Lady and Betty still said nothing.

"Reclaim my mystic," I bellowed from the kitchen door. I followed it with more shouting and some door slamming, which had as much affect as a cup of water tossed into the Sahara desert.

Even The Daughter of Ramses Two was unmoved. She slept through the whole tantrum, friggin' purring.

A few days later I sat in Steven and Sheryl's kitchen, with a lot on my mind – mainly that retrieving the scrapbook was completely point-less as they had probably already read it. And, from the sounds of Steven on the phone, were hardly affected by it. Perhaps I had been a tad over the top, that The Bag Lady was right? That my Beryl Story was the equivalent of a blog post that no one read but merely click 'liked'.

Just stick to the script I told myself now: menopause, sex and how belly dancing helped me. Maybe a little something made up to add a bit of mystic to my belly dancer persona...

Steven was silent.

I was ashamed of my past, it is as working class as a Mars Bar, and yet it boiled inside me, compelling me to tell all.

Shut it, I told myself, *stick to The Change.* Keep people guessing about the rest.

Steven sat for ages, stirring his coffee, and to be honest it was either scream at him to stop it or, well, talk. And before I knew it I was cutting open my soul. Once I started I couldn't stop, my words erupted, burst forth, dispelling the mystique I had built around myself. Soon I was talking of my shit past, a story not even fit for a soap opera. It was a bit like lancing a boil.

Steven was that good a listener.

The funny thing was, Sheryl appeared a few days later with a gift voucher for a posh hairdresser in Glasgow. She called me brave. I must have looked shocked because she also gave me a hug.

"I know you're not the huggy type," she said, "but I just wanted to give you one. I had no idea of what you've been through."

I said nothing, but that hug was the best. I didn't want her to stop.

The last time I had a hug Rodger was still straight.

Chapter Twenty

FABULOUS YOU

The Bag Lady and Betty made old age seem like an adventure

Sheryl

That night after Neff left, Steven and I decided to look through The Bag Lady's scrapbook, despite Neff claiming that her "innard thoughts" were in there and were for Steven's eyes only. He had a real thirst for folks' stories, which I guess is the writer in him, and he wanted us to do it together, over a dram. I was curious too – listening to the recording of someone spilling their guts can do that to you – and anyway, it reminded me of sitting around the campfire, The Bag Lady reading tea leaves and Neff calling it a load of rubbish.

The first time I saw The Bag Lady she was obviously homeless. No one knew where she spent her nights, some said the graveyard. She was sitting in front of the Co-op, singing off key with her organ on full Ghetto blaster volume. She was screeching to drown out the traffic when folk walked by without a coin toss. Then she moved to playing outside Neff's bookshop. Everyone wanted rid of her, not Neff. She and Rodger were going through their break up at the time and taking in The Bag Lady seemed to help Neff, especially when Rodger insisted on selling the bookshop and Neff had no choice but to comply.

At the time I thought Neff was mad. The Bag Lady was not the sort you'd want to sit to close to, on account of her hygiene. I had passed her many times, always holding my breath. No matter how big a garden I had I would not want her and her pile of old skulls and crappy bath mats in it. Neff, however, took her in without a blink, without one brag, like it was the most natural thing in the world to clutter up your yard with a teepee and a permanent campfire. It took me years to see there is more to The Bag Lady than smelly socks and an ability to mess up Neff's garden.

Neff talked about her being an agony aunt and a reporter for a local newspaper, something the Bag Lady never denied but didn't expand on either. One time, Neff had even shown me a photo of her, a red-haired woman looking, Neff claimed, like Lucille Ball, (whoever that was). We were standing in Neff's kitchen at the time and The Bag Lady walked in, caught me oohing and aahing, and with a snatch of the photo retreated to her teepee. I heard she gave Neff a mouthful later, claiming that her past "was not Neff's to share." According to Betty it took several spliffs to calm her down.

When Steven opened the scrapbook now, it was to a glamorous fifties-style photo of a short red-haired woman staring into the camera without a flinch.

"Wow,'" he muttered, and turned the page with reverence; it crackled heavy with newspaper cuttings. He turned another: more photos, and letters glued in.

It was like an art student's workbook.

Steven continued. On page after page, there were bundles of notes, and postcards stapled to corners, pages covered in scribbles, sketches, and comments; more cuttings, letters...Creativity gushed forth like a broken tap.

Some of the letters were from her columnist days, as Deirdre-the-agony-aunt, in a '70s magazine called *Fabulous You*. Alongside each problem was The Bag Lady's answer, as witty as Ms Frasier's description of sex and as insightful as, well, The Bag Lady still is. I turned the scrapbook towards me, and read:

Dear Artful Dodger,
I have not printed your letter as I feel the names of body parts used out of

context are inappropriate for readers of this page. But let me just reiterate, I did not suggest that to overcome your obsession with stealing, you should adopt a Robin Hood stance.

Please stop handing out PlayStations nicked from Oxfam shops to children in the park, no matter how bureaucratic you think Oxfam has become. It is not legal. And please stop handing out sex manuals to the Seventh Day Adventists. It's not funny, and as far as I am aware they are still capable of having sexual relations without any instruction.

It was one amongst many. We pored over the scrapbook, read the entries, gazed at the photos, and chuckled, turning the tea-stained pages slowly, until a single photo fell out. Steven picked it up.

"I'll never look at her the same again," he said, handing it to me.

A teenager Deirdre stood on a riverbank, holding up a "just caught" fish, and a Julia Robert's smile. Scrawled on the back was date, along with "Dad and me".

I wondered, as I often did, what had happened to her, how she ended up in Lochgilphead so alone and why she no longer wanted to be called Deirdre? Did she ever marry? And who on earth told her she could sing, let alone play that god awful organ. Neff did ask, about the name and got a mouthful from The Bag Lady.

"I want to be free from my past," she'd shouted. "It is enigmatic and *I* wish to remain that way." She was sober at the time too.

She never plays the organ now. She'd stopped the time she sang "Smoke On The Water" after one too many spliffs. The noise was particularly bad that night as she attempted a few seventies guitar riffs on the organ.

It was the evening of the photo-snatching, when me and Neff were in the kitchen, trying to work out why The Bag Lady would want to hide her photos. The next thing I know Go Boy's hurling himself over the fence, followed by a rolled-up newspaper.

We charged into the garden to find The Bag Lady thumping Go Boy with the organ, Jason shouting at the dog, and the fence a shambles, flatten on the ground.

Her organ never played a note again. The Bag Lady left it abandoned in Neff's lounge, hidden under a pile of belly dance books and josh sticks. After a while, Neff polished it up, set it on its legs and now uses it as a sort of shrine to her "turning her life around".

While I day-dreamed, Steven turned the final pages. At the back of the scrapbook Neff had added a few sheets. Hers were neater; no scribbles or drawing but legible writing, with photos and newspaper cuttings glued in an orderly fashion: cuttings of her, her belly dancing troop, and a woman called Beryl. According to Neff's words, Beryl:

"Changed my life. Inspired me to rise from my loneliness to feel again and take belly dancing to a new level.
An invisible, ordinary woman, whose only ability to stop traffic was when she misread the traffic signs properly.
Who not only persuaded me to part with fifty quid, but attend her act –
The Fortunes of Tomorrow with Madame B."

It was accompanied by a photo of a middle-aged grandmother, who was poured into leather tight enough to make breathing hard work. *This* was the woman who Neff described as...

"Mesmerising.
With each trancelike breath, Beryl's chest heaved that bit more, making the men sitting in the front row happy to toss their coins into her pot.
I watched, learned and absorbed every trick. Beryl had nothing more going for her than a decent chest and a lot of balls. If she could do it, so could I. If she could hold an audience, why couldn't I?
Inspired, I decided never to be a student again. I was going to take my chest, my hips and all that I learned from Beryl back to Britain and find a way, like Beryl, to have an audience eating out of my hand."

"I wonder what had happened to Beryl," was on the tip of my tongue, when Steven turned the page.

It was covered in clippings of The Taj, all with Tenzam poised like he had just been caught out: in the kitchen mid pot-stirring, in the yard mid mobile-shouting, by the car mid depositing-a-carry-out, by the table mid customer-chatting, and outside with a jaunty wave.

Steven looked at me. "Has Neff got a thing for Tenzam?"

"Hardly," I said. "He's way too young."

"He's not that young."

"He's in his twenties, isn't he?

"Forties," said Steven, "according to Neff."

"Wow." I looked more closely at the photos. "I guess a curry really is the fountain of youth."

Chapter Twenty-One

THE SECOND HAIR CUT

A Mystic is just another name for a Magician

Sheryl

A week later Neff appeared with a new purple Cleopatra haircut.

Helen and I had spent the morning attacking Mum's garden. Helen and I are not really gardeners, we run our own "no job too small" DIY business. And even though Helen is nothing like my tough-as-old-boots sister Lindsey, Mum treats as her daughter.

Mum, it seemed, was sick of looking out onto her overgrown garden and, despite Neff's suggestion of a gardener with a six pack, had roped Helen and me into it.

Mum was desperate, she wanted a tidy up before Ms Frasier, "mouth of the north" appeared. How Ms Frasier got involved I had no idea but apparently she was due to arrive with an azalea and the anticipation had set Mum into a panic.

I might have mentioned Ms Frasier had a habit of taking over. It was the Army in her, which gave her illusions of mission impossible schemes with her at the helm. She was a frustrated captain yearning for a project and once she found one she was as unstoppable as the flow of my mother's criticism.

"The last thing we need is her offering to plant the thing," fretted

Mum. "Before you know it my garden will be a tribute to *her* Australian outback – full of eucalyptus trees and kangaroo gnomes." Mum *was* prone to exaggeration, except when it came to Ms Frasier, we had all seen her in action and knew what she was capable of.

Helen and I had arrived early, almost sunrise, and were in the garden, just sipping our "let's make a start" coffee, when we heard a loud "Cooee."

Before Mum could shout, "Dive, hide, run for cover," Ms Frasier appeared, pushing a wheelbarrow full of cuttings from her garden and a luscious pink azalea. She had the look of someone who planned to stay and plant the shrub herself, immediately setting Mum into a spin.

"We're done for," she muttered, and then spent the morning playing deaf to Ms Frasier's, "Australia's azaleas are the size of emus and as bright as a galah," comments.

Helen, who is never good at ignoring people, said a polite, "Really?" several times, sending Mum into a spasm of teeth-grinding and "shut it" looks, which led only to even more "Reallys" from Helen.

With spades and shears, the three of us filled our wheelbarrows several times: tidying up, weeding and pruning, while Mum watched, with her "this is my garden" stance, waving her trowel around like a conductor's baton and the occasional "not that one" comment.

Not that Ms Frasier took any notice.

Mum has always been resistant to advice, let alone being taken-over, which Ms Frasier did with such goody-two-shoes, I-know-best energy, so Mum was soon at bursting point, the sort which leads to sarcasm of the highest level and mass exaggeration. It wasn't long before she was wheeling herself about the garden in a frenzied fashion, shouting of "mass destruction" and "decimating", which no amount of quiet, "It's just pruning, Mum," could quell.

The entrance of Neff and her new Cleopatra look was a godsend.

I had just lobbed the remains of a brown clematis into the wheelbarrow and, with satisfaction, was casually dusting off my hands, when Mum reversed her wheelchair to my side.

"You've killed it!" she hissed, almost spitting in my ear. "Shaved it to the bone. It will never live to rise again–" She stopped, catching sight of Ms Frasier attacking a past-it's-best rhododendron with a spade. Mum's face flushed – a shout was on the horizon – when Neff came into view with a nonchalant walk, as if she had always gone about as a geriatric Cleopatra.

Mum dropped her trowel. She stared, the rhododendron forgotten. "What the blue friggin' blazes..?" Mum wore her hair short, and sniffed at such things as highlights and perms, despite the fact that she had regularly succumbed, sporting a sort of poor-man's Joan Colin's bouffant look. Lockdown changed that. Once she saw what her hair was really like, she went natural. Blessed with thick hair and the sort of curls that just bobbed into shape, she quickly became sniffy over those who spent hours at the hairdresser, even when cursed with thin, tired, old hair.

Helen threw me a "here we go" look.

"Where did you get that done?" yelled Mum, like Neff was miles away.

"Where?" Neff said. "A small place in the West End."

"West End of Beirut?" Mum sneered.

"A very posh establishment in Glasgow," Neff continued. "Care of your daughter."

"Was purple her idea?" asked Mum.

Oblivious, Ms Frasier huffed the rhododendron into the wheelbarrow and continued to dig.

"And do you know what the stylist asked me?"

"Are you colour blind?" guessed Mum.

"Am I over sixty-five?" Neff looked from me to Mum to Helen. "Me, she asked me if I'm over sixty-five?"

"But you are, aren't you?" Mum frowned.

"She's sixty-three, Mum," I said.

"Sixty two..." snapped Neff "...and eight months."

"Oh, I thought you were more my age," muttered Mum.

Ms Frasier stood up, wiped her brow and looked down at a hole the size of a grave. "Perfect" she muttered.

Helen nudged me, as Ms Frasier pushed the offending rhododendron to the "burn later" bonfire heap, dumped it on top and pushed the wheelbarrow to her car.

"I could have slapped her," snapped Neff.

"Two years is hardly a slapping offence," said Mum.

"Two years and eight months."

"Same thing, isn't it?"

"Try telling the pension people that," said Neff.

Ms Frasier reappeared pushing her wheelbarrow, now carrying a knee high eucalyptus tree and a small clay platypus gnome. "Neff has a point, Beatrice," she said put in as she passed, "to a young person you're a fossil at fifty."

Mum's eyes were on Neff, she seemed unaware of Ms Frasier. "Why would she want to know your age?"

"She said if I were a few years older, I'd get a discount – enough change from my voucher for a dry cut."

"It's a retirement thing." Ms Frasier grunted. She dumped the eucalyptus into the hole. "Like at Specsavers. Apparently once you reach sixty-five you can't afford full price. Why not just put an "Old Git" sign up? "If you're over the age of shagging then please let us know and we'll give you ten percent off to cheer you up". Huh."

"I'm not over the age of shagging," muttered Mum.

"Exactly." Ms Frasier huffed, shovelling dirt around the eucalyptus tree. "There is no age limit to shagging."

Helen nudged me with a, "What's with all the shagging?" look.

"Why can't people just lie?" said Neff. "Pretend to be surprised when I say my age. I do it all the time."

"I can always tell when you lie," I told her.

"A tiny white lie never hurt anyone. Give me an "I thought you were younger" comment any time but sod off with your "thought as much". Who needs to hear that?" Neff sighed. "What wouldn't I give for just one more, "Aren't you still in your fifties?" Just one friggin' more."

"Hence the purple." Mum's muttering got louder.

"Pff." Ms Frasier started patting the eucalyptus into place. "My hairdresser is mercenary. The last time I was there she had me as past it as that rhododendron I just chucked..."

"You *chucked* my rhododendron?" Mum turned on Ms Frasier.

"...There I was, sat in front of the mirror complaining about the amount of hair left in my brush. And she looked at me like "old is for aliens" and I was one of them. Young folk never think age will happen to them. I know I didn't."

Mum reversed her wheelchair to the "burn later" bonfire pile, and wailed, "My rhododendron!"

Ms Frasier stood up to admire her bush. "She lifted a hair strand – like it offended her – and said, "I've seen worse," as if that was gonna make me feel better. "It's the shaft," she said. "Once it goes grey it gets thinner. But dyeing it helps, it thickens things"."

"Enter purple.' Mum poked her rhododendron.

"Apparently, along with a free Over Sixties bus pass comes a skin so thick, insults bounce off it." Ms Frasier dusted off satisfied hands.

Mum uselessly tugged at the branches. "I thought there was still a bit of life in her."

Ms Frasier threw a look at Mum. "There is more than a bit of life in me."

"Sheryl," shouted Mum, ignoring her, "have you seen this bonfire pile?"

I didn't say anything.

"It's like a plant sale."

"A lot of them *were* past their best," Helen tried.

"Ageing isn't great," said Neff.

"My poor plants." Mum shook her head. "Decimated."

"I try not to care and yet I do," said Neff. "Years ago when I walked past a shop window I saw my mother's face and now it's my friggin' granddad's."

"Did your grandfather have purple hair too?" Mum yelled.

I sent her a "give it a rest' look.

"And there is nothing you can do about it," Neff went on. "You can try to hide it under make up, clothes–"

"Hair dye." Mum again.

"–but still you're old."

"I may be in my eighties," said Ms Frasier, "but I still get about, do things. Even have sex." She dumped the platypus by the tree.

I looked at Helen, *she's having sex? A woman who referred to men as dribbling drongos, who had as much change of getting a "stiffy" as George fitting into a leotard.*

Ms Frasier stared at the platypus as if she'd said nothing odd. "Although I do it with the lights out now."

"With the lights out?" Mum repeated. "How do you find your lubricant?"

Chapter Twenty-Two

MS FRASIER

Loneliness is in the eye of the beholder

Sheryl

The thought of Ms Frasier having sex had me gobsmacked, she just didn't look the sort.

She looked the sort who saw it as her duty to pick up litter and volunteer to drive people to hospital. The lonely sort that talked way too long at the supermarket checkouts and bored people stupid at Council meetings. Ms Frasier, with her legs in the air, seemed as likely as, well, my Mum having sex – not a vision I wanted to conjure up.

Mum had done her best to gain some ground with sarcasm, but a sexually active Ms Frasier had her stumped, lost for words. Stupefied, she blankly watched as Ms Frasier disappeared and reappeared, with a wheelbarrow carrying outdoor solar lights and a collection of Australian-themed garden gnomes, koalas, kangaroos, emus, even a dingo. Where the hell she got them from was any ones guess but still they kept coming.

"Oh, yes, it's sex in the dark now for me..." she reminded us as she tipped the contents of her wheelbarrow, with a crash, onto the grass. "Everything's gone south and who wants to see that? "

A dingo had landed on its back, its rigid legs stretching skywards like comic rigor mortis.

Neff bent to right it. "Oh I know," she muttered.

"I'm bald in all the wrong places," added Ms Frasier.

"Tell me about it," Neff agreed.

Ms Frasier produced a bag of knitted gnome outfits, lacquered and waterproof.

Helen and I watched as Neff helped her dress the animals, as if it was the most normal thing to do. Even the Phrygian caps were knitted and lacquered to the stiffness of a cricket bat.

I wanted to ask where and why but Ms Frasier hellbent on discussing sex was like a tsunami of words – shagging being the main one.

"My pubic hair went with my teeth," she said.

"Oh god, me too." Neff sighed. She placed a cap on the dingo.

"I've the pubic hair of a coconut on chemo," proclaimed Ms Frasier, disappearing to her car.

"Exactly," yelled Neff. "What is the point of a happy pelvis if the family jewels aren't properly dressed."

Ms Frasier reappeared with a large scruffy-looking hut. Still talking, she stuck the joey inside and began to arrange the other so-called gnome statues around the hut like an Australian naivety scene. "My equipment stretched to the point it's not keeping things in. I can't laugh without a leak. And as for sex it's like parking a moped in a garage." She stood back to admire her handiwork. "Sitting on top is a total no go."

Helen looked at me. "Who's *she* having sex with?"

Ms Frasier turned to us. "I've had my flings, don't you worry."

"Flings, in Lochgilphead?"

"Not here…A woman goes away for such things." She went onto to talk of a very small, very dexterous man from Crieff who made gnomes in a shed so small you could heat it with a "lit match."

Which would have had us all laughing if she hadn't added, "And there's more than one way to sit on a gnome."

Normally Neff would have butted in, gone on about her hips circles keeping everything in good working order, but engrossed in the positioning a kookaburra on top of the shed she said, "A fling at my age is as possible as *this* kookaburra building a nest."

"This is about Tenzam's wife, isn't it?" I said to Neff – anything to change the subject.

"Or *that* kola climbing *that* eucalyptus tree." Neff gave a disheartened gesture.

"I've heard she's very young." I was fishing.

"I don't think it's his wife," Mum chimed in. "Have you seen her" She's the spitting image of Tenzam."

"The Roadworks Man says it is. His wife,' said Neff.

"Pff, what would he know? He always getting things wrong."

"It's the dark skin and all that coconut oil." Ms Frasier was heading back to the car with her wheelbarrow. "Takes years off a face."

"I thought they used ghee," said Helen.

"On their faces?" I said.

"Ghee is for posh cooking," muttered Neff. "They use mustard oil."

"On their faces?" I repeated.

Neff said nothing.

"The Aborigines use emu oil." Ms Frasier reappeared with a statue of an emu and several clay parrots in her wheelbarrow.

"Oil from an emu?" said Helen.

"And those people never age..." said Ms Frasier. "You think they're sixty and they're a hundred and three, still tossing boomerangs."

Mum turned from the compost heap with a sigh. "Nobody cares about my age, they just see my friggin' wheelchair and try not to put their foot in it."

Chapter Twenty-Three

THE GARDEN

A nativity scene doesn't always need a manger in the Garden

Neff

To say Ms Frasier talks way too much is like saying a politician lies, it's a given.

I've seen her about the place, holding up queues at Tesco's checkout, the petrol pumps, not to mention stopping people in the street. People pull a wide berth when they see her coming like she's got the latest Covid. Stopping Ms Frasier mid flow is like trying to stop soap suds oozing from a leaking washing machine. Once she opens her mouth the only thing to do is run. In fact, that was what I was planning to do when I saw her and her friggin' wheelbarrow – run before anyone saw me.

Then she started talking of sex.

I had no idea she could be so fruity, let alone sexually active, I just thought she played bridge – badly; Beatrice was always going on about it.

Anyway, Beatrice did her best to gain some ground with sarcasm and I got a few good lines in, but Ms Frasier held court. At times it was even funny, comedian funny. I even wished Mavis was there, she'd have chuckled, she definitely would've enjoyed the coconut joke. I did, until that is Ms Frasier moved on to her hairdressers – and lost her audience.

Completely unaware of our glazed expressions, she worked through all the hairdressers she had "sat under" who had, "clipped her like a merino", "shaved her like a convict", and "permed her like an eighties soap star". She'd been through more hairdressers than Madonna's been through looks and young men. By the time she was on what must have the tenth, she was claiming the stylist had "the tack of a three-year-old".

"...She probably had Asperger's," Ms Frasier was saying. "It's rife, you know, every man and his dog has it these days. Some blame vaccinations. I blame the food – the other day I was walking past the veg section in the Co-op and I saw a carrot so big you could knock a bull unconscious. I mean, that's just not natural."

I drifted off.

Beatrice was looking at her phone, Sheryl started dead heading a geranium, while Helen was topping up everyone's mugs from her flask, which, surprisingly enough, wasn't something hot but rather a chilled smoothie with, I suspect, a hint of rum. I sipped mine, thinking about exactly how much rum was in it and could I get more, when something caught my eye under the hydrangeas by Beatrice's back door.

It was an impressive bush with branches bending under the weight of its pink puff ball flowers. How it had managed to escape pruning by the ruthless Ms Frasier was beyond me, it had so many flowers they were trailing on the ground, hovering about the back door, catching any leg that passed. As I watched, there was a shudder from beneath, a rattle of branch, a fluttering of petals...

I heard a squeak.

A mouse dashed from underneath.

A paw shot out, knocked the mouse from its feet, then Puss appeared.

Puss watched the mouse scurry to its feet, sitting as she always did, small, clean, and cute, hypnotising you to pat her. She looked so innocent, as if she had no idea what a mouse was, and I was just pondering whether to bend down and give her a chin tickle when...

Slap.

Her paw crashed down on the mouse stopping it in its tracks.

Ms Frasier's voice filled the silence. "There's me sitting in the chair, telling that hairdresser how marvellous Australia is, how they have the lowest rate of Aspergers in the southern hemisphere and she, without even letting me finish says, "Why don't you move back there, then?" Imagine."

The mouse squeaked.

Puss pawed the mouse with the cool interest of a predator; she let it go and it

made another dash.

Slap.

The mouse was silent, still.

Puss scuffed it sideways.

The mouse didn't move.

Puss rolled it about like a marble.

The mouse flopped, its little paws trembling in a prayer pose.

Puss stared like she was waiting for it to move.

The mouse twitched, made to roll.

And Ms Frasier bellowed, "And before I had a chance to answer she started to tell me how she was brought up there. In Perth. How she still kept in touch, had all these friends and family out there, how they visit each other all the time. How her father moved back and it was the best thing ever." Ms Frasier shook her head. "I couldn't get a word in…"

"I find that hard to believe," muttered Beatrice.

Puss launched into the mouse's head with her teeth. I heard a squeak, a crunch of bone then Puss looked up. She caught my eye, freezing mid crunch with a "what the fuck do you expect? I'm a cat" look, and returned to her kill, diving in with gusto.

"…When I finally did, I told her that I'd be lonely if I moved out there, I'd have to start again, make new friends. She gave me one of her "what are you talking about" looks, like lonely didn't exist in her world, like loneliness wasn't even a word. "Do you not have any friends?" she actually said." I turned to see Ms Frasier staring at her handiwork, brushing imaginary dirt from the kangaroo's nose.

No one said anything, not even Beatrice.

It was a long time since Rodger had left, but I still remembered the loneliness. People ran a mile. Sheryl threw me an embarrassed smile.

Predator Puss licked her paws like butter wouldn't melt, the mouse demolished to a small dot of its innards, as if it never existed. She sidled up to Ms Frasier, and wrapped around her legs, pretending the only thing that had been near her lips was a cat biscuit.Ms Frasier bent to pat Puss. "She was cheap and quick but still, is that any excuse to, well, you know, insult?"

"I hope you didn't tip her," I said.

Beatrice wheeled herself slowly over to Ms Frasier's outback scene, and said, "Nice work, Ms Frasier, thank you."

"Definitely," said Helen.

"Absolutely," said Sheryl,

"I'd sack that friggin, hairdresser," I added.

"Fuck the hairdressers," said Beatrice. "Go natural like me, you'll never look back."

Chapter Twenty-Four

BEATRICE

The best jokes comes from a listener

Neff

I watched Ms Frasier fuss a bit more over her Australian outback scene, I was seeing her in a new light. She didn't seem the sort to care what anyone said, let alone a hairdresser.

"I've been to hairdressers like that," I told her. "Maybe you should come with me – to *my* hairdresser."

She looked right at me. "Your hair is the colour of an aubergine."

"What's wrong with that?"

"My hair is white," she explained. "Not that it has always been that way but, well, white is better than grey, don't you think?"

And before I could answer she launched into a monologue about hair colour and her ancestors.

It took me back to my first day with Steven; he gave me the lecture of the century. He started out with, "An artist listens and observes before creating." And before I could tell him I was the listener of the century he launched into the sort of monologue that belongs on TED Talks. "Like you do with music," he cryptically added.

"I know that–"

"Feel, listen, and interpret."

Like I had never thought of that before.

"You must do it with people; try to understand how they feel, what motivates them."

"I am aware of–"

"In order to write their story." He looked at me. 'You did ask for me to mentor you."

Now, staring at Ms Frasier, I suddenly understood what Steven had been talking about. I wanted to know more, to put Ms Frasier in my book – and I told her that. Her face lit up like a Christmas tree.

"You have so much to say." I meant it. "And such a way of saying it. Why don't we do a recording?"

She gave me an even bigger smile.

"For my book, perhaps, even a podcast?" The podcast was just a shot in the air, I had no idea how to do one but when Ms Frasier clapped her hands with delight I wondered if I could learn about them.

"Shall I bring my wheelbarrow?" she asked, with an impish grin.

I chuckled, wondering if the others were finding her as funny as I was – and then realised they had all disappeared. Sheryl and Helen were in Beatrice's garage "putting things away" while Beatrice, herself, had disappeared upstairs to her kitchen, peering out the window now and then.

I walked Ms Frasier back to the car. I didn't have to, but I wanted to and she didn't stop talking even as she jumped into her car and turned on her ignition. I slid in beside her, bowed to the unstoppable flow of Ms Frasier's tongue.

This was a woman with a story to tell.

Chapter Twenty-Five

GNOMES

You can't put experience on a pair of young hips.

Sheryl

When Mum heard about Neff and Ms Frasier she was a bit miffed.

Not that Neff was subtle, with the voice of a fog horn, she asked Ms Frasier for an interview like it was a great TV appearance.

Several feet away, Mum's face dropped. "Don't you want my story anymore?" she mumbled, and before Neff could answer (not that she heard, she was too busy with Ms Frasier) she reversed away from the "waiting to burn" bonfire heap and headed into her kitchen to clatter and crash about.

The kitchen is my mum's retreat, a place where she takes her anger out in chopping things. Soon she was huffing over the slow cooker, dicing up onions for an Army, and when she ran out of onions she moved with a vengeance onto the carrots, claiming she was "cooking for the soup kitchen."

I had no idea there was a soup kitchen in Lochgilphead.

Neff and Ms Frasier left soon after that. With a quick "we're off" shout at the bottom of Beatrice's stairs they disappeared like bosom buddies, while Helen and I cleared away the tools and then carried up logs up for the fire in mum's lounge.

We had just dumped the last batch when Mum appeared at high speed. She parked her wheelchair beside the couch and was getting ready to slide onto it when George appeared with a door slam.

"The garden looks great, Beatrice," he yelled from the bottom of the stairs.

Mum paused, mid move. "You think?".

"Yes. Just met Neff with Ms Frasier. She says a few more gnomes and it will be ready for the competition." He huffed up the stairs, appearing a little flushed at the lounge door, clutching a bottle of his favourite malt whisky. "I didn't know you were entering the garden competition."

"Neither did I," said Mum. "I just wanted my azalea planted. Wish I never bought the thing now."

"I thought you won it in a raffle," said Helen.

"The raffle was *her* idea." Mum grunted. She resumed transferring herself to the couch, using the sort of arm push-up that had me marvelling at her strength. "That woman is as loyal as a hungry dog stranded in a room with his comatose owner."

George rolled his eyes at me. "She has done you a garden worth sitting in.' He gestured to his whisky bottle. "Drink?"

"Like a hungry dog," Mum insisted. "One lick to the wake owner, one twinge of hunger pain and the hand that fed the dog has been demolished." She landed with a soft thud. "Apart from the finger nails."

"Bit bloody, Mum," I said, immediately regretting it.

"Bloody? *Bloody?* The only thing bloody is that woman's treachery."

"I think you might be over egging the whole thing," dared George.

"And it was her idea to dress me up in egg boxes," yelled Mum.

"You loved it at the time," Helen pointed out.

Mum grabbed the remote, and with a glare at the TV, began to angry channel flick.

"I thought you'd be happy to see the back of them both?" I said. "No more Neff and her nagging you for your story."

"Yes, well."

"No more Ms Frasier and her wheelbarrow," Helen added.

"I am over the moon!" Mum snapped, stopping at re-runs of the Queen's funeral. She turned up the volume.

"And I thought you hated the Queen," said George, grabbing the remote.

Chapter Twenty-Six

AN AUDIENCE WITH MS FRASIER

A performer is only as good as her audience

Neff

I decided to record Ms Frasier by the bonfire, using the "Steven Technique". I did think about working with him again but from the look on his face when I mooted it, I decided not to. Mavis said it was putting unnecessary strain on his and Sheryl's marriage, that the couple already had a lot to content with.

To be honest, she shamed me saying that, although I'd never tell her so.

I figured that if we were in the garden and Ms Frasier's motor mouth ran away with her, The Bag Lady and Betty could hem her in, and if they couldn't, I could escape inside; slipping away from Ms Frasier in full flow would be as easy as kicking off a slipper.

A few days later, on time, Ms Frasier appeared.

The Bag Lady, in pensive mood, greeted her with a grunt. She was cheesed off with Ms Frasier invading *her* space, and was as sulky about it as a grounded teenager. All morning she moaned on. "I'll be lumbered with *that* woman when you've had enough," she said. Then she bribed Betty to stay as long as necessary.

It was only then I heard The Bag Lady mention the stashed hash.

"If you want our hash kept a secret you're friggin' staying to the bitter end," she told Betty. "Right til that woman is talked out and has shuffled off."

Betty shrugged. "Who cares?"

"What do you mean," The Bag Lady sounded outraged, "*who cares?*"

"Nobody bothers about hash these days, smoking a spliff is as mainstream as a pint of beer."

"What do you mean, mainstream?"

"Everyone does it." Betty gave another shrug. "No one gives a toss about you and me and what we smoke."

"I'm sure Shifty does," The Bag Lady said. "The last thing he wants is a stoned mother."

"Pff, him? He's all taken up with that garden competition. He and Rodger have turned my beer garden into a Shakespearean themed affair. So random."

"Random?" muttered The Bag Lady. "What do you mean, *random?*"

"Oh you know." Betty huffed. "So *yesterday.*"

"What's got into you," said The Bag Lady.

"Rodger has done up my beer garden like some sort of Shakespearean theatre with the two of them gadding about in tights and codpieces. It's enough to put you off your scrambled eggs."

"Nothing puts you off your scrambled eggs," bitched The Bag Lady.

"My son in a codpiece does. And they've pulled out my geraniums for their so-called Elizabethan herbs."

The Bag Lady looked unconvinced. "And where did they get all these so-called Elizabethan herbs from?"

"Tesco's in Oban."

The Bag Lady started to laugh then and Betty followed. Soon they were plotting how to use the remains of the stashed hash; when I heard "yoga" I left. I didn't want to know any more about their yoga under the influence. I had a garden to tidy up, and the last thing I needed was another outback nativity scene to look at while bubbling in the hot tub.

Ms Frasier, minus her wheelbarrow and plants, finally appeared after what she called the "meeting to end all meetings," which none of us wanted to know about. She told us anyway. "The so-called Committee For Social Development – who are supposed to be planning the garden competition – want gnomes banned!" Ms Frasier had, she said, called them politically incorrect "and a lot more" and so sparked a riot of swearing from the Community Project Lead, who claimed the garden competition had always been "plant based".

Janice MacGregor, who owned the hardware/garden store was, to quote Ms Frasier "flabbergasted" and completely on her side; she had just shipped a truckload of gnomes in for the competition and "was expecting to make a killing". The Community Garden Project Lead was having none of it.

'We're talking compost heaps and carrots," he'd yelled – causing a full-blown outburst from Janice MacGregor, who roared back that compost and the like was as profitable as selling cat biscuits.

"Though half the meeting claimed a tad tasteless." Ms Frasier paused, caught her breath and before I could rush in with, "Fancy a drink?" she launched into another speech. Describing The Community Garden Project Lead as a thin man with way too much hair for his own good, she acted out the meeting. Even The Daughter of Ramses Two seemed hypnotised.

'He put up a good fight," Ms Frasier admitted, "holding the floor like a Pentecostal preacher and extolling the virtues of teabag compost and happy snails like they were the answer to global warming. But then, "Who cares about friggin snails," yelled Janice MacGregor, with a tirade about small business and local economy. A pet peeve of hers. I couldn't get a word in," said Ms Frasier – one of her favourite sayings and a true testament to her ability to exaggerate.

By now The Bag Lady and Betty had disappeared into the teepee. I could hear them chuckling. Ms Frasier was undeterred.

"There is more to a garden than vegetables, I told them." She nodded vigorously. "And Janice Mc Gregor backed me to the hilt. You can tell she's a true gardener by that red outdoorsey face of hers."

"I think that's more to do with whisky," I muttered.

"Gardens are for sitting in in and enjoying," said Ms Frasier. "I mean, take yours..." She stopped and gazed around, clearly taking in the meditation pyramid covered with The Bag Lady's hole-ridden socks pegged to it; the rubber bath mat by the teepee entrance, with "Women Only" scrawled across it in felt tip pen;, the wobbly fence care of Go Boy's constant jumping at it; and The Daughter of Ramses Two perched on the corner of the hot tub looking like a regal buddha.

She shoogled the pyramid. "You could get rid of these socks," she suggested. "Set up an Egyptian sort of thing."

"Over my dead body," yelled The Bag Lady's voice.

"As for the tent…"

The Bag Lady poked her head through the flap of an entrance, smoke billowing from behind her, and glared a Ms Frasier. "What?" She coughed.

"Remove the tent, place a porch here—"

"A porch?" snapped The Bag Lady. "What the frig do we want a porch for?"

"For when it rains," Ms Frasier explained. "And put in a chimenea—"

"A chimeny-fucking-rea?" The Bag Lady was yelling now.

"It wouldn't take long," said Ms Frasier. "You could get Sheryl and Helen to help. Sort that fence at the same time."

Go Boy barked.

"How about we start on your story?" I raised my voice, catching the dark look on The Bag Lady's face. "Let's start with your childhood."

"That fence is just fine how I fixed it," The Bag Lady muttered.

"If Sheryl and Helen are busy I could do it," offered Ms Frasier.

"Where were you born?" I shouted.

"I spent hours on that fence." The Bag Lady plonked herself down beside me. "It's just fine as it is."

"I've got a few gnomes, still. We could Egyptian it up with a bit of paint," said Ms Frasier.

Betty's face appeared at the teepee flap. "You can't Egyptian up a gnome."

Go Boy barked again, and Ms Frasier cocked her head. "We could sort that dog out, and paint Egyptian figures on the fence. How about I come back tomorrow? We could make a start."

"If she's coming tomorrow, I'm staying away." Betty coughed again.

"And I'm coming with you," snapped The Bag Lady.

Ms Frasier stopped, sniffed the air, caught sight of The Bag Lady's face, and demanded, "You on the weed?"

"No."

Ms Frasier started to laugh. "Any left? It's been years."

Chapter Twenty-Seven

THE BONFIRE

The deflowering of a woman has nothing to do with petals

Neff

A few hours later, the bonfire was a mere glow of embers, the hot tub was bubbling away and all three of them were in it, sporting the sort of underwear a woman wears when she's celibate and spring cleaning. They were calling their evening, The Underwear Festival. I was inside, in my one piece swimsuit and dressing gown, rustling up sandwiches and hot chocolate, while they called me chicken.

"Show us your bra," shouted Ms Frasier, sparking Go Boy to a frenzy of barking; a frenzy stopped by the tossing of a ham bone.

The three of them had bonded over sex (again), or rather the talking of it, and to be honest it was getting a bit much. I mean, I thought I'd lived a little but my exploits seemed quite tame compared to what they said they'd got up too. It also turned out that the stashed hash was way more than a few leftover spliffs and they were knocking it back like teenagers at a proper festival.

Not me.

I've never smoked the stuff after that fried egg incident a couple of years ago. After a session involving moonlight belly dancing to Bob Dylan (only possible when stoned) I'd headed into my kitchen with the peckish feeling only a fry up could fulfil. The next morning I woke to find my kitchen splattered with egg yolks and tomato in a variety of forms, my bin full of egg shells and empty tins of tomatoes and my egg spatula melted onto a hotplate I'd never use sober. The Bag Lady had filmed it all on my mobile: me cooking, while attempting to perform the Dance of the Seven Veils with tea towels.

Tonight I, spliff free was playing host, trotting back and forth to the hot tub with trays of drinks while the three elderly women mellowed under the moon, and The Daughter of Ramses Two peering from the under the flap of the teepee entrance with a slightly scared look.

Betty inhaled then passed her spliff to The Bag Lady.

"I was eleven when Mother gave me the sex talk to end all sex talks." She coughed. "The sort to scare any orgasm out of me."

"Eleven?" scoffed Ms Frasier. "I was in kindergarten."

"And she did it in one sitting," Betty added.

"No one gave me *the* talk," said The Bag Lady. "I learnt it all from the school's toilet wall."

Betty took another drag. "It was the early sixties, the pill had arrived, and Mother feared for my virginity. She grew up on a diet of Doris Day films and "don't do it until you're married" sex advice."

"Didn't we all?" said Ms Frasier.

"There were no virgins were I came from," said The Bag Lady. "The only virgin they knew came from a bottle of oil."

"Young people were challenging everything," Betty carried on. "And Mother feared I'd join them, turn into a tart and end up like Marilyn Monroe, who according to her, "got what she deserved"."

"That's a bit rich," muttered The Bag Lady.

Betty sucked on her spliff. "'You ever wondered why cats's bottoms are different?" she said."

"Who me?" I asked.

"Shh," said Ms Frasier, which had me and The Bag Lady choking on our hot chocolate.

"Even at eleven I knew that it was not only weird to look at a cat's backside but to call it a bottom. Mother talked of male and female "cat's bottoms" like she was explaining the Theory of Gravity and I couldn't even spell the word. Like it was the most natural thing in the world to stare at such an orifice."

The Daughter of Ramses Two looked up, and almost silently meowed.

The Bag Lady called to her.

The Daughter of Ramses Two didn't move.

"I remember our cat was parading up and down at the time, her tail in the air almost daring me to take a peek." Betty shook her head slowly. "I must have glazed over because Mother, in her best scary voice, moved onto the evils of men, claiming they were all like un-neutered tom cats, spraying their seed with no regard. "Testosterone, rages in their loins rendering them incapable of reason, it's up to us women to keep a wide birth," said Mother. She was beginning to sound like Billy Graham, and I was seriously scared. Apparently, even sitting in the cinema would court the sexual act, if I wasn't vigilant." Betty looked at The Daughter of Ramses Two. "I remember trying not to look at our cat, doing that cleaning between her legs thing in a way only a cat gets away with."

As if she understood, The Daughter of Ramses Two continued to ignore The Bag Lady's, "Come here," and started washing her ears.

"Mother was going through her born-again phase which, to be honest, never really ended" said Betty. "Only virgins get the man of their dreams. Once you've lost that you may as well go to a nunnery, no decent man marries a tart", she mimicked her mother's voice."

I stared at The Daughter of Ramses Two, the only cat I had ever known that never did that cleaning between the legs thing. Perhaps she did it in secret?

"My Mother called it deflowering. She said, "a man will talk you into bed, promising the moon, then run away quicker than a rat up a drainpipe." She said they could smell a woman of no virtue a mile away." Betty sighed.

"Blimey, even my Mother didn't talk like that," said Ms Frasier, "and she was a staunch Catholic."

"The fear lasted for a year or two until the boys I knew were old enough to drive and I was old enough to stay out past the early evening news. I soon learnt that the myth of virginity was as dead as Mother's petticoat. Sex, well almost sex became a weird mixture of fear, guilt and confusion."

"Teenage fumbles in the cinema." Ms Frasier laughed. "I snogged my way through just about every Elvis Presley film."

"I remember a campsite experience involving the accidental demolition of an ant hill and some very angry ants," mused Betty.

"*I* remember a sandy fling on the beach that lived up to the myth that dark men had big penises," countered Ms Frasier. "It was so big it had me running back to the hotel and drowning the sight with a lukewarm Pepsi."

We all laughed at that. Ms Frasier was encouraged:

"The chances of that tree trunk fitting into my insides was as possible as parking a lorry into a Wendy house," she said.

"As if," joked The Bag Lady, jumping out of the hot tub. She wrapped herself in a towel and sat down by the fire.

"You could hang a week's washing on it," Ms Frasier insisted. "Not that I told anyone. Finally I met a young man with a manageable size penis and very few words. His father owned a shop that sold everything from fuse wire to biscuits in large tins. He used to deliver for his father in a van and tried to "deflower" me in more ways than you could skin a cat. He called it exploring my "Milk Tray". He had a thing for chocolate." Ms Frasier sucked on her spliff and passed it to me, I handed it to The Bag Lady. "His metaphors were as bad as his fumbling, so remaining a virgin was as easy as resisting a bag of Liquorice Allsorts. Despite the discomfort of his gear stick and my resistance he never gave up."

"That was the summer of sex fumbles in secret." Betty jumped in. "And sneaking back to a nocturnal mother with love bites hidden under a polo neck jumper." She sighed. "The summer of guilt."

"Tell me about it," said Ms Frasier.

"No matter what time I came in, Mother was upright in bed, Dad snoring by her side, her face glistening with Ponds cream, and an "I can read your mind" glare. Her bedroom was right by the front door, it was impossible to shuffle past, especially when the door was wide open."

She faded into silence.

The fire crackled.

"All that holding back, what a waste," Betty added after a while.

The Bag Lady handed her what was left of their spliff and called The Daughter of Ramses Two again. The cat finally gave in, padded over, and curled up on The Bag Lady's lap.

Chapter Twenty-Eight

THE LEAN-TO

A lean-to has little to do with leaning

Sheryl

Helen and I were in The Taj when Neff walked past, looking particularly smart for a stroll in Lochgilphead. I was leaning against the kitchen doorway, mid hot flush, while Helen was in the kitchen with Tenzam. He had ideas for a better kitchen and seemed to think Helen and I could work miracles. She was doing her best to be optimistic.

The kitchen was smaller than a two man tent; how The Chef cooked in it was a miracle of breathing in. No wonder the guy was skinny. Only two people could stand in it at a time and even then they were so close you could tell if they had cleaned their teeth.

Tenzam's teeth sparkled straight and white, I noticed, as he talked about the need for more bench space for packing and plating up. *In this egg box of a place—no chance,* I thought.

The kitchen consisted of a sink the depth of a grave, a tandoori oven also the depth of a grave, an ancient, scrubbed within an-inch-of-its life gas hob with six hob burners and a shelf above groaning with black seasoned-to-fuck woks and pans. Beside the sink was a bench the size of a chopping board with a pile of unruly receipts and above was a microwave, precariously perched on a shelf that had been erected by someone with no idea what a spirit level was.

I'd always thought Neff was exaggerating about the place but if anything she'd toned down her descriptions. I peered out the window after her, but there was no sign. *Where was she going, done up like that?*

Helen, however, was seeing hope under the sink.

Tenzam bent to look, wafting aftershave and garlic my way.

"Packing under here?" he said. "This is not possible."

"No, I meant you could store stuff under the sink, perhaps clear that bench and...Hmm." She stopped, catching sight of the lopsided shelf.

The Chef shouted something at Tenzam. He, now on his second fag had spent the last hour parading the backyard while talking on his phone with a voice louder than a lawn mower. Tenzam looked up, hit his head and rubbed it. When he stood up, receipts fluttered to the ground.

Helen pulled a tape measure from her pocket and looked at me. "What about a small extension?"

Tenzam lifted a box from the top of the microwave and with a broad sweep of his arm filled it with the receipts. He dumped the box under the sink and then glanced from Helen to me. "What is this extension?"

I was just about to answer when I heard a woman's voice behind me, speaking in Bangla. I turned to see a tiny Asian woman, who I assumed was Tenzam's wife. She peered past me into the kitchen and handed Tenzam a mug.

"This is Hia," he said while jiggling the microwave open.

Hia was nothing like I expected. I'd thought she'd be more...well, "sari-like", at least wearing a headscarf. Hia wore nothing on her head. She, dressed in jeans and a dark jumper with her black hair in a bun, looked more like someone from Glasgow than Bangladesh. She saw me looking and threw me a smile – just like Tenzam's.

Tenzam slid the mug into the microwave and flicked it on.

"Or maybe a lean-to would work,' Helen was muttering. She gestured at the backyard. "We could move benches out there."

"Benches outside?" said Tenzam.

"It will have a roof," Helen explained.

The microwave pinged. Tenzam slid the bubbling mug out and, bypassing my head, handed it to Hia.

Helen eyed the bubbling mug. "We could move the microwave out there, too."

"You need a dishwasher," said Hia.

"I told you, there is no room," Tenzam replied.

"But with an extension." She looked at me. "Could this be possible? Next to the sink?"

I didn't know what to say, neither did Helen. I mean there are miracles and then, well, there is mission friggin' impossible. The backyard was pretty much taken up with a shed that was already bigger than the restaurant. It was full to packed with an American extra large fridge, a couple of freezers, sacks of onions, potatoes, rice, and flour all piled about the floor, in every place possible. All the shelves were groaning with large jars of pickles, boxes of veg and herbs, and even more pots and woks. Outside the shed was an array of empty oil cans, a couple of bins, and a coal bunker for the tandoori oven.

The Chef dropped his cigarette stub, ground it into oblivion and placed his phone in his pocket. He had the look of someone who wanted us to leave his kitchen so he could come inside. I asked Tenzam if The Chef was angry, and he laughed.

"No, he is waiting for you to go into the restaurant, he wants to make you lunch."

Lunch? I looked at Helen, and my stomach rumbled. *I could really go a curry right now* I thought. I was starving.

"How much is a lean-to then?" said Hia.

Helen, a woman who could make something out of nothing, came up with a price that stopped me in my tracks.

"Er, is that possible?" I started, distracted again by Neff walking past the front of the restaurant. This time she wore enough make-up to shame a drag act.

"Where is she going?" said Helen, "all done up like that.'

I shrugged. "Maybe she got a gig somewhere and decided to put her make-up on first."

Chapter Twenty-Nine

EXPECTATIONS

Expectations are often as realistic as a set of false eye lashes

Neff

I was just walking past The Taj, expecting to see it in darkness, when I caught sight of Sheryl, casually leaning by the kitchen door, lights blazing around her, and looking completely at home. I couldn't believe it; The Taj was closed on a Monday. What was Sheryl doing there and without telling me? She told me everything. I mean, we were like sisters.

Well, she can just get stuffed, I told myself. Not meaning a word of it.

I peered closer…And then I saw *her*…Tenzam's wife.

My heart almost stopped, my chest froze, my stomach tightened to a golf ball size of pure acid. She was so friggin' young, way younger than I imagined. I could easily be her mother or, god forbid, her grandmother.

I watched as she stood behind Sheryl, stretching an elegant arm over Sheryl's shoulder, all casual like. She was so slim, so tiny, with a waist that not only looked good with a belt but needed extra holes for the bleedin' hook. The sort of waist that meant a corset was obsolete and made any man feel like The Hulk – even Tenzam and his tiny hands.

She moved about the restaurant like an Algerian woman balancing a pot. It wasn't a walk, or a march, or a strut, it was an exotic glide that any belly dancer would give their right shimmy for. It was so smooth she could balance a chamber pot on her head and not spill a drop. I have seen many walks in my time, *performed* many, but none compared with hers. It was like she was born to glide, like she had glided from her mother's womb without a hint of afterbirth, and then friggin' glided to her mother's breast.

Not that I was jealous or anything.

I stared at my reflection in the window. My fringe casually fluttered across my forehead, exposing the grey my hair dye missed. My frown was so like my mother's, and I had an army of forehead wrinkles, care of my friggin' grandfather.

I felt clumsy, stupid, and old. Exactly like the first day I saw my pink hair sober.

I just need more make-up, I told myself. *Darker eyeshadow, perhaps redder lipstick.* I was half-convinced, just in the middle of reassuring myself that the local chemist would have such miracle make-up, when Sheryl looked across and almost caught my eye.

Jesus.

I moved on.

Let them crack at it, I lied to myself and turned to head back to the car. Why should I bother who was doing what with whom? The Taj had nothing to do with me and yet...and yet...*I really wanted to know.*

The Bag Lady says I am a busy body, but I'm not really, except, well, for Tenzam, *there was something about him I couldn't put my finger on.* Sometimes I fantasise about making his life better–

Well, I did. With a wife in the picture, the last thing he'd need was my help

I stopped, knowing I should make for the car, head home. Yet I lingered, swithered. Perhaps I could go to the chemist first, check out their make-up, or maybe some eye cream? I headed up the next street; I *really* needed some eye cream. I passed the Red Cross shop a few doors down from The Taj – and stopped again. Before I knew it I was inside, trying to look interested in their clothes.

The Red Cross shop was not the friendliest of places on a Monday, probably because Monday was She-who-lives-to-Moan's day.

She-who-lives-to-Moan had once – just once – been to one of my classes and then complained of backache ever since; like I had personally jumped on her back, broke her spine, and kicked her kidneys all the way to Aber-friggin'-deen.

I was poised over a red eighties jumper that belonged in the recycle bin. *Why did I feel like this, so...so...hurt, like I did when I saw Shifty hold Rodger's hand?*

Was I jealous?

Mavis says so but then she likes line dancing and Zumba; *I could hardly take her seriously.*

She-who-lives-to-Moan looked up from her till. "Going out are we?"

"I'm working," I lied.

"Oh, I thought perhaps you'd been dancing." She gestured to my face and mouthed, "The make-up."

I picked up the red eighties jumper, held it against me and stared at my reflection.

Stop thinking, I told myself. *You're not jealous you're just out of sorts.*

She-who-lives-to-Moan threw me one of her fake smiles. "That's a size ten," she said. "The eighteens are over there."

I slid it back on the rail. Normally I'd give her a mouthful but I couldn't be arsed even giving her a look.

"Were did you get your hair done?" she said in a neutral tone.

I told her.

"Did you get a refund?" and before the insult hit me she asked what was going on at The Taj.

"I have no idea." I eyed the toiletries shelf.

"There's a lot of shouting about their shed, and it's putting me off my sorting," said She-who-lives-to-Moan. She threw me a 'can't you do something about it' look which I chose to ignore.

I picked up a lavender soap and sniffed it.

The Red Cross, being a few shops down from The Taj, shares the large green behind it and their own shed – like The Taj's – is full to bursting. Only theirs is full of second hand gear. According to She-who-lives-to-Moan, Monday is their busiest day, their sorting day, on account of people dumping bin bags outside the door despite the "No Leaving Bags" sign.

"People become illiterate at the weekends," she says. "Reading signs is apparently a weekday thing."

I replaced the lavender soap and lifted a Lilly-of-the-valley, immediately regretting a sniff.

She-who-lives-to-Moan started to talk of the Garden competition and how they would like to enter, to raise, as she called it, "Red Cross awareness".

"There are a few in it already," she said.

"Oh?"

"The theme is nativity."

I nodded like I didn't know, like I hadn't seen it on Facebook, like I hadn't spent an afternoon with Ms Frasier, who went minute by minute through each committee meeting since their conception.

"Of course, it's the manager's idea not mine. I mean, with my back I can hardly water a pot plant, let alone dig." She threw me another look. "And I can't see us having any chance with them a few doors down." She took me outside and gestured to The Taj's yard, like I had never seen the back of the restaurant before.

The Chef, perched on a convenient log, spat out his cigarette then continued to talk on his phone.

"Could that man *be* any louder?" She-who-lives-to-Moan said.

"He's not that loud."

"Pff, a pneumatic drill is a whisper compared to him. And just look at the mess."

"There is only two of them," I reminded her. "What do you expect?"

"The other day I arrived to find a pakora skid right across my entrance. One false move and my disc would have dislocated right up my backside." She huffed away, with a pronounced back rub.

"I don't think that is possible," I said.

"Well, it is when you skid on a pakora. Just ask Ms Frasier – she was there, grabbed me just as my heel made contact with a rather nasty-looking piece of chicken."

I caught sight of Helen appearing from the back of The Taj,

clutching her tape measure. She was deep in discussion – thank god – before she looked my way I headed back inside the Red Cross, making my way to the bookshelves, wondering which were Mavis's leftovers.

She-who-lives-to-Moan moved from skid marks to pet dogs and the odd cat. I pitied her poor husband. Ms Frasier says he is so frightened of leaving skid marks that he's constipated, and has a panic attack at the mere mention of a curry.

"Hey, would you mind keeping an eye on things?" She-who-lives-to-Moan shouted from the Red Cross shed.

Which had me heading out the door quicker than I could sneeze.

One more quick walk past The Taj, I thought. *Just one more look.*

Chapter Thirty

FOOD

One woman's hunger is another's flat stomach

Sheryl

Helen and I sat in the restaurant, listened to the sound of frying, and waited.

Tenzam, Hia and The Chef not only managed to fit into the kitchen but to cook together with more talking than a radio talk show.

"Can I help?" I shouted.

No one answered.

I peered into the kitchen to see an intensity of action on a par with disarming a nuclear bomb. The cooker had all six gas jets on full. The Chef was chopping at the speed of light. Hia, with the focus of a surgeon, stirred and shoogled pans, while Tenzam was virtually in the sink, scrubbing like his life depended on it.

I returned to Helen, the fragrance of spices now teasing my stomach into the sort of lustful hunger you feel before a Christmas lunch. She gave me a patient smile, as we waited and waited listening to Bangla music on full volume. Eventually, Tenzam poked his head around the door.

"Tea?" he offered. "Or coffee?"

We nodded giving our orders.

Tenzam disappeared to the kitchen, then reappeared placing a mug in front of each of us.

"You like spice," he asked.

I wanted to scream *I'll eat anything* but nodded politely with Helen, as he disappeared again, with an airy, "Won't be long."

I sipped my coffee, my stomach making noises, as we watched folk outside walk by.

Helen looked serene. I wanted to eat the table.

An eternity later Tenzam appeared again, carrying a jug of water like it was nectar from the gods. He placed it on the table. "You like chilli?" he asked.

Chilli? I was seriously contemplating the paper napkins.

He vanished back into the kitchen and the frying continued, followed by a loud burst of laughter as my hunger peaked to a faint mouth-watering feeling.

Tenzam poked his head around the door. "You like music?"

Helen nodded an enthusiastic, "Yes," as a hot flush hit me like a sledgehammer and I fanned my face with a beer mat.

Tenzam slid his small round body behind the counter. He's a short man, shorter than me with little hands and feet, and a round smiley face that looked younger than his forty-odd years.

Hia joined him, hunting for napkins or whatever moving with an upright confidence like she could balance a plate of spaghetti on her head and not spill a drop, even if she sneezed. She's even smaller, younger-looking than Tenzam, with the sort of flat stomach I'd give my right kidney for.

Just bring some food, I wanted to shout.

Instead, I watched Tenzam choose a Bangladeshi song.

The Chef began to sing along, the frying stopped, and a few minutes later, Hia reappeared with a bowl of salad chopped into colourful slivers.

My mouth watered. *God I was hot.*

Helen laughed at my face. "Not long now."

"I'm past caring." I gulped the last of my water and was just about to top up our glasses when The Roadworks Man appeared from nowhere and pulled up a seat like he was invited.

"Have I missed anything?" he said with a robust napkin flick.

I was too faint to answer.

Hia appeared, with a bowl of plain rice and a bowl of coloured rice. She threw The Roadworks Man one of her Tenzam-like smiles and went off *again*.

"That'll be the wife," whispered The Roadworks Man.

Tenzam and a pile of plates, washed and dripping, arrived at the table. He polished each plate to a shine then placed one in front of each of us, The Roadworks Man included. The Chef appeared, on cue, with a pot of dhal. I sniffed, peered and drooled, my mouth so wet it could fill a teapot.

I don't deal with hunger well; I'd be the first to eat roadkill in a famine. I think it comes from a hungry childhood and a mother hell bent on having a skinny daughter.

According to Mum I was always the first at the table, knife and fork poised for eating, and to teach me patience I was the last to be served.

I felt like that child now, waiting with a shrunken prune-like stomach with its sides stuck together. *How long must this torture go on for?* I thought.

The Roadworks Man was watching me. "It's worth the wait," he promised.

Hia brought another bowl, overflowing with succulent looking aubergines, and another of hard boiled eggs perched on a bed of juicy fried onions. Tenzam followed with a tray of pickles and stopped to top up the jug of water.

"All homemade." The Roadworks Man observed.

Who cares, I wanted to scream. *I just want to eat.*

The Chef served a chicken dish, Hia a plate of chillies, and Tenzam went back for serving spoons.

Finally...*finally*, they sat down and gestured for us to start.

"Wait," said Hia. 'We forgot the fish."

For fuck sake.

They ate efficiently with their hands – The Roadworks Man, too – mushing the curry into the rice, moulding it into a ball, then sliding the ball onto their tongues without a drop spilled. I made far more mess with my fork. As my stomach began to relax into a delicious full-ness, the last of my hot flush subsided.

I looked up to see Neff, passing the restaurant yet again. This time, Tenzam saw her too. He jumped up and dragged her in, gave her a plate, and before we knew it she was tucking in, also expertly using her hands like she had done it all her life.

Tenzam turned to Neff. "This is Hia."

Neff nodded, mashing an aubergine into her rice with a little more force.

"She is here for a few weeks, for a conference."

Neff stopped. "A few weeks? I thought *she* was going to live here."

Hia looked confused. She spoke in a soft, easy to understand accent – The Chef and Tenzam called her Babi. "Live here?" she said. "Leave my sons?"

"You have children?" Neff was looking at Tenzam. "I had no idea you were a father."

Tenzam laughed. "I'm not a father." He glanced between Neff and The Roadworks Man.

The Roadworks Man stared at his plate, meticulously forming the last of his rice into a ball.

I cleared my throat. "Is Hia not your wife?"

"Hia is my sister," explained Tenzam.

Neff gave The Roadworks Man a look. "I thought you said he was bringing his wife here?" The Roadworks Man blushed.

Tenzam laughed again. "I have no wife."

The Roadworks Man slid the ball of rice into his mouth and wiped his chin. "A man can get things wrong now and then," he muttered.

Neff leant back in her chair with a shrug. "An easy mistake, I suppose." She sighed.

The Roadworks Man stopped mid-wipe. Normally, we all knew, Neff would make a meal of it, give him what for. Not this time. She actually looked quite happy.

"He always gets things wrong," Tenzam said to his sister. "He has the hearing of a squid."

Helen asked Hia about her conference, while I gulped water; my hot flush returned with a vengeance.

"It's a women's conference," said Hia.

"Hia is a doctor," Tenzam informed us.

"You don't look old enough," I joked, fanning my face with a beer mat.

"She's an expert on healing foods." The Chef cleared his plate with a wipe of his hand. He licked the juices from his fingers with relish. "Hia is the head speaker."

Chapter Thirty-One

HIA

To assume can often led to missing out

Neff

There I was, passing The Taj, minding my own business, when the next thing I knew, Tenzam dragged me inside the restaurant and I was tucking into the sort of food that makes conversation a trial.

The aubergine delight was inches from my mouth when Tenzam comes out with, "Hia – she's my sister."

I nearly choked. But then, when I looked at them closely it was as obvious as The Roadworks Man's overalls with "Roadworks" in fluorescent capital letters on the back.

Tenzam and Hia were almost identical.

Not sure why, but I could have kissed The sheepish Roadworks Man. Of course I didn't. I didn't do anything because I realised as I looked at Tenzam what I really wanted to do. I, well, I...wanted to shag him stupid!

A man more than ten years younger than me, who looked at least twenty; a man earning less than a boy on a paper round; a man that saw me as a mature, white lady who drank too much – he had no idea about the past dope exploits. I was so shocked with myself, I even left my aubergine. That had Tenzam confused.

"Is there something wrong with the aubergine?" He said.

I said nothing. I couldn't take my eyes off Tenzam's lips; I had never noticed how plum they were. *Stop it, forget it,* I told myself.

I had to go.

Before they got up to make tea, I made my hurried excuses. I was almost out the door when Tenzam caught me; his delicious aftershave wafting my way.

"Can you help tonight, Neff?" he said. "We have a party booking."

I looked around the shed of a restaurant and wondered if it was a party for toddlers. His sweet face was sending me weak at the knees. I nodded. "Okay, but I can't stay too long."

His face lit up, while my stomach sank like a shoe full of bricks.

Working in The Taj was as intimate as sharing a bath, and my face burned at the thought. A whole night with him and his aftershave. I grabbed a beermat from the counter and began to fan my face.

Sheryl called over to me. "I thought you were past the menopause?"

Tenzam turned to me with a quizzing look and I could have punched her. Instead I scowled and was just working on an answer that wasn't too sarcastic when Tenzam smiled at me and said,

"Neff, your hair. It is very nice."

Chapter Thirty-Two

THE PARTY BOOKING

There is more to spice than chillies

Neff

The party booking was, as Ms Frasier put it, "The inner nucleus of The Community Garden Project Committee." Or as I would put it, a table of five hell bent on getting pissed before Ms Frasier arrived.

The table of five took over most of the restaurant. With his back to the wall was he Lead, an elderly Andy Warhol look-alike with silkier hair that flopped over his eyes like a wet flannel. He was new to the area and new to The Taj and from the look on his face not a curry lover. To his right and looking as perky as a sixteen-year-old on her first date was McTaggart's wife Isobel. A woman who, according to Ms Frasier, had "come out of herself "once her husband retired.

After the very humiliating nose-diving of his pop-up library. Mr McTaggart, surviving an ingrown toenail operation, claimed he could no longer give his all to his job and assumed his long-suffering wife would join him. He was taken aback when she joined the Community Garden Project Committee instead. According to him she'd never looked at a plastic flower before, let alone the real thing, and had as much interest in gardening as she did in his ingrown toe nail.

The Lead, according to Ms Frasier, welcomed her with opened arms – and more. A lover of horses and of all things organic, he had introduced Isobel to enriched manure that could bring life to a bowl of sawdust, the joy of worms, compost bins, and dirty vegetables that made stock so tasty she tossed her stock cubes to the wind. She remained, though, on the fence about gnomes.

Sitting opposite them on the table for five, was Janice MacGregor, who stared at the menu tight-lipped, and the "art teacher-cum-garden entrepreneur", McFlaherty. He was a flamboyant man with Braveheart hair and a way too tight frilly Elizabethan shirt, which he claimed added a certain, "Je ne sais quoi" to not only his art classes and but his gardening.

"I can't wait to sink my teeth into some decent butt-clenching chilli," McFlaherty said, casting his eye over Tenzam's small rear.

Whether Tenzam was aware of any butt-gazing it was hard to tell as he was in waiter mode, clutching his pad and pen, poised for action. "You ready to order?" he asked.

"We're waiting on someone," said The Lead.

Isobel looked up from her phone. "She says she'll be here in five."

"Ms Frasier's five is at least ten," muttered McFlaherty.

"Ms Frasier?" Tenzam looked at the spare seat, then at me. "She is coming?"

"Yes.' The Lead sighed. He glanced around his colleagues. "And there'll be no more talk of gnomes."

Tenzam disappeared to the kitchen and returned, placing a large plate of poppadoms in the middle of the table. "On the house," he said.

McFlaherty stretched across, his Elizabethan frills wavering above the spicy dip.

"Mind!" gasped the entire restaurant.

McFlaherty laughed, extending his reach without contact. Years of frilly shirt wearing had made him a spatial-awareness expert. He ran his-life drawing classes in such shirts, painted in oils wearing them, even dug about his garden, his frills ruffling in the wind and enough buttons open to reveal a pretty lick-able chest, and never was a stain to be found.

Ms Frasier finally appeared when I was in the middle of opening the third bottle of bubbly. As the cork popped, she pulled up a seat gasping. "I'm sorry I'm late – compost emergency." And before you could say "poppadoms" she launched into her story.

It was a story so long the nucleus of four had sculled way too much bubbly and were mumbling about "shorts" – whisky and vodka – while Tenzam was like a cat on a hot tin roof. A second table booking had appeared, took one look at Ms Frasier and ordered a takeaway, and Janice MacGregor and McFlaherty had turned to gnome jokes, and there was still no sign of ordering.

Tenzam turned to me with an expected "save the day" look.

"You ready to order?" I removed the empty dip dishes.

Ms Frasier continued speaking. She had a story of slugs and snails to finished and barely stopped for breath. She didn't acknowledge The Roadworks Man's arrival, talked louder as he scraped his seat into position, and even louder when he, with a cough, opened his beer. Like magic, the kitchen door opened and "the staff Jalfrezi" filled the restaurant with an aroma that would tempt an anorexic. Tenzam appeared, plate in the air, as if he was holding a masterpiece – which the staff Jalfrezi truly was – I followed with the rice, naan, salad, and chef brought a plate of bubbling dhal. Each was placed reverently in front of The Roadworks Man.

Ms Frasier stopped mid slug pellet recommendation, and with a look of pure lust turned to Tenzam. "I'll have what he's having," she said.

"Me, too," chorused the others. Apart from The Lead who, with a sniff, ordered fish and chips.

It wasn't long before they were all tucking into their food, and even Ms Frasier stopped talking. Isobel was giggling at everything The Lead was whispering close to her ear, like they were sharing personal jokes.

"You really are the limit," she cooed, placing a tender hand on his shoulders.

"Am I?" whispered The Lead.

Isobel slid her hand onto his thigh without even trying to hide it.

Ms Frasier gestured to me with a flamboyant naan wave. "This is Neff, my friend," she announced.

No one said anything

"She's writing a spectacular blog."

"Book," I said.

"With me in it." Ms Frasier shoved a bitesize chunk of naan into her mouth.

"And other women," I said.

"It's all about the belly and pelvis," Ms Frasier mumbled with a full mouth.

"And other things," I said.

Ms Frasier swallowed hard. "Men and women," she said.

Isobel threw a fruity look at The Lead.

"There's more to my book than that," I said.

"But mainly sex." Ms Frasier's voice was way too loud.

I turned to Tenzam, wondering if that was how he looked when he was uncomfortable.

"She going to interview Hia," said Ms Frasier. She licked her fingers.

Tenzam looked at me quizzically and I blushed; it was the first I had heard of it.

"We thought she was Tenzam's wife, turns out she's his sister."

Isobel stopped nuzzling The Lead and turned to Tenzam. "You're alone, in Scotland?"

"I'm not alone," he said.

"You have a girl, then?"

"Well, no."

"Oh. A boyfriend?"

Tenzam shook his head, then started to collect the dishes. He nodded at me to help.

"Leave the poor guy alone," Janice MacGregor snapped at Isobel.

"But he's alone," said Isobel.

"Let's just park that thought," said The Lead. He turned to me. "Perhaps we could have the bill?"

"No one should be alone," slurred Isobel. She glanced at The Lead.

"I am happy," said Tenzam, with a weird look at me.

"I'm sure there is someone..."

"He said he was happy, Isobel," said Ms Frasier.

"Never give up. I didn't."

"We can see that," muttered Janice MacGregor.

"Look at me, I'm over sixty..."

The Lead hushed her. It didn't work.

"We could fix you up with someone," Isobel went on.

"I don't think he needs fixing." McFlaherty caught my eye.

With a blush I stretched for a plate.

"I know a nice girl, Polish. She takes care of my neighbour," Isobel offered.

"What's Polish got to do with it," asked Janice MacGregor.

"Or maybe it's Russian..."

"Russian?" McFlaherty raised his eyebrows. "Here in Lochgilphead? Who the hell is that?"

"She lives in Ardrishiag, actually," said Isobel.

"Same thing," muttered Janice MacGregor.

"No it's not," said Isobel.

"Let's just agree to differ," suggested The Lead.

"There is a three miles difference," snapped Isobel.

"Shall we split the bill," said The Lead.

"Anyway, it doesn't matter." Isobel looked sadly at Tenzam. "The thing is that she's away from her family and so are you."

"My sister and brother are here," Tenzam told her.

"And she's so hard working. She could help you in the evenings."

I looked at Isobel. Punching was too good for her.

Chapter Thirty-Three

EWA

An accent can mean many things

Neff

The so-called Russian that Isobel was offering Tenzam was a young carer called Ewa. She was actually an Italian who had spent many years in South Africa, which seemed to have seasoned her already rich accent.

She arrived at The Taj three weeks later, during lunchtime – which meant me standing/sitting about, just in case someone came in while The Chef prepped for the evening. I don't usually work lunches except when Tenzam rings out of the blue.

That morning I was plonking food into The Daughter of Ramses Two's bowl and she was looking at the bowl like yesterday's scraps, then at me as if I should be ashamed. She disappeared with a silent meow just as Tenzam rang. He needed to pick up supplies in Oban and Hia wanted to join him.

Standing in the empty restaurant, I was pondering the constant changes of a pregnant cat; that morning's *weird reaction for a feline so passionate about chicken, especially when it was her favourite dark bits*. I wondered if their hormones were like ours: did they have only so many eggs and go through The Change? These and other such intellectual thoughts were going through my mind when Ewa waltzed in like she owned the place. She was followed by The Roadworks Man – someone who *never* appeared until well after the evening news – and they were laughing together like they'd spent their youth pub crawling and had just met up to relive the memories.

Ewa, who said she had been helping the Red Cross "pretty up" the outside of their shed, was looking way too clean for outdoor work; when Sheryl worked outdoors she ended up looking like a coal man. And The Roadworks Man was in his funeral get up – having just been to one – and had been heading home to change, when he came across Ewa, "Welding a spade like a true navy", as he put it. "She'd put half us roadwork men to shame."

Ewa laughed a truly annoying laugh. "But you boys use machinery now."

Her flirting was way too obvious for my taste but The Roadworks Man lapped it up. I watched her delicate hands run down the menu, wondering how she managed a spade, and was just going to make a food suggestion when Tenzam and Hia appeared.

Within seconds they were all chatting, like they'd grown up together and been to the same school, while I, pen and pad poised, was standing behind the counter, like an old invisible idiot.

You'd think Ewa and Hia were joined at the hip the way they immediately got on, and *she – Ewa –* flirted like mad with Tenzam. There was something about her accent, her Madonna-like ego, her flamboyantly chatting-up anything with a pulse (apart from me) that really grated on me...or was it the *apart from me* that grated?

Hia seemed to think it was all brilliant, but then she would, wouldn't she? Hia, according to The Roadworks Man, was keen for her brother to marry someone who would make it easier for him to stay in Scotland. Tenzam didn't seem to mind either, he even gave Ewa *that* smile – the smile I thought was just for me. *Why should I care,* I argued with myself, *it's not like I'm contender. She's way more his age.* And yet I did – care, that is.

"Try the staff curry," The Roadworks Man said to Ewa.

I could have punched him.

"Yes." Hia eyed her approvingly. "And why don't you sit with us."
"And me." The Roadworks Man pulled out a chair.
I was so riled I could have spat.

Chapter Thirty-Four

CAPTAIN BIRDS EYE

Years of teaching belly dancing gave me a repertoire of fanny jokes that could rival Joan Rivers.

Sheryl

It had been three week since Helen and I surveyed The Taj. In that time we made a few sketches and had erected a roof, which was almost finished. All things considered, it was looking good.

At night I went home to hear the latest from the Neff recordings, and was learning a lot – mainly what you think people are, is nothing like how they see themselves. Ms Frasier had opened up to Neff, leaving the sort of recording that had me feeling sorry for her. Loneliness, it seemed, was her best friend, until my Mum got the bit between her teeth.

For some reason my mother was really fired up about the Garden Competition.

I'd barely heard of it till now, and hadn't known this Community Garden Project Committee existed, but this week Mum's talked of little else. Even Ms Frasier was taken aback by her ruthless energy. George says it's the tennis grand slam all over again: Mum played any sport going until the stroke left her in a wheelchair, but tennis was her favourite. She was as competitive as John McEnroe in his heyday and just as devious. She won every cup in the region – mostly by analysing her opponents, listing their weak points, then exploiting them to the hilt.

Now she was doing the same with the Garden Competition. The theme was "Nativity with a twist" and whether it was Ms Frasier's outback onslaught on her garden or Neff subsequently befriending Ms Frasier, I have no idea. But Mum, it seemed, was both desperate to win and desperate for Ms Frasier to help.

That morning I walked into Mum's kitchen expecting to find Mum peering out the window over her usual morning coffee, and found Puss, alone, poking at her cat biscuits. She turned to me with a silent meow, made for my legs, and commenced her "I want a pat" leg-wrapping.

"I'm in the operations room," shouted Mum.

Puss purred closer. I picked her up and headed to where I could hear Mum and Ms Frasier – in the spare room. In just a few days they had amassed pictures from most of their competitors and it was an impressive sight. I had no idea there was such imagination in Lochgilphead, especially when you think the prize was just a mention in the local paper and a trophy to sit on your shelf for a year. Mum had her spot all ready, smack in the middle of her mountain of tennis trophies.

I looked around the "operations room", normally a place for drying washing, stacking old newspapers, and house plants on their last legs. Right now, there was not a pair of socks or a pot plant in sight, just photos of Mum's competitors tacked on the walls, and Ms Frasier and Mum so busy they merely grunted a "Hi' over Radio Scotland faintly playing in the background.

Ms Frasier was mid pinning up a photo of Shifty and Rodger's Shakespearean beer garden, and Mum was wiping the remains of the destruction of the pop-up library project from a whiteboard, with the sort of ferocity I hadn't seen since the days when she polished her sports trophies.

Stroking Puss's warm body I looked over the photos, some giving Ms Frasier's Australian outback a run for its money, others offering more of a good laugh.

The Bowling Club had put together a traditional Santa sledge riding into the Wild West. The nearby organic farm had constructed a Celtic fairy garden out of recycled cans, wellies and organic veg, their compost heap as the centre piece. There was no tinsel in sight and their fairies, according to Ms Frasier were "as magical as a loo brush."

The nursery's Disneyland Christmas garden was more childlike, all painted stones and pink stick figures dotted about a few shrubs. It was the sort of display, quickly knocked up by an over-worked assistant, that only a parent would be proud of.

The Council Headquarters Garden was equally thrown together by another over-worked, under paid public servant, a part-time gardener, who as Mum put it, "Had the imagination of a colouring-in enthusiast and as much chance of winning as her compost heap."

The retired vicar's garden was a Highland Clearances theme, complete with starving gnome children clustered around a fire. A theme Mum claimed, "Turned the anti-gnome brigade on its heels," and Ms Frasier called innovative, yet poignant. For once Mum didn't argue. Finally, Gordon who ran the chippy had created a Birds Eye Fish Fingers garden using pot plants, plastic fish with movable singing heads and a Captain Birds Eye dressed as Santa Claus, waving mechanically.

"It's hardly Christmas material." Mum sniffed, and to prove her point had stuck the local paper's scathing review underneath the photograph: "A few plant pots does not make a garden," it read. "So unimpressed am I, I can't write any more. Please remove the garden and give us more chips with our cod."

"If Captain Birds Eye is Santa Claus, then I'm a mink whale," Mum said. "And if Birds eye Fish Fingers are a Christmas treat then my bunions are a laugh a minute."

"You've been busy," I said.

"I know. Ms Frasier is a demon, she did all this." Mum glanced about the room.

"Apart from the review," said Ms Frasier. "You wrote that, Beatrice."

"We're in with a chance," said Mum. "We just need a photo of what that Red Cross shop is up to."

"The only real contender," Ms Frasier agreed. "I heard it's little Red Riding Hood bringing a stuff turkey to her grandmother. Although no one's sure what plants they have used. I mean, it's hardly a garden out the back of that shop."

"That place is a dump." Mum was busy admiring her clean whiteboard.

"The fishmonger says they've used the hedge..." Ms Frasier stepped back to look at her photo.

"Hardly a hedge," muttered Mum.

"....and sculptured it into Chipolata sausages."

"He's having you on," I said.

"I believe Little Red Riding Hood is a rewired bonsai that someone handed into sell," Ms Frasier went on.

"As if," I said.

Mum swung her wheelchair in my direction, just missing my feet, and making Puss jump from my arms. "We're counting on you," she told me.

"Me?"

"You'll be at The Taj today."

"Yes, but I'm working."

"You can still take some photos."

"I said I'm working." I turned to Ms Frasier. "Why don't you do it?'

"Because I'll blow my cover," she said.

"What cover?"

"The cover that gets me half price size sixteen dresses."

"You're a sixteen?" I looked at her slim waist.

"Well, that's what that so-and-so in the Red Cross shop says."

"If you're a sixteen then what's she?" Mum had a caustic look at my round menopause stomach. "Twenty?"

"Curvy." Ms Frasier gave me the sort of smile that made me say, "Okay, then. I'll do it."

Helen laughed when I told her and was laughing even harder when I stood outside The Taj and stared across the back of the Red Cross shop. A huge tent covered the length of the green behind it and barricading the tent was a clothes line full of clothes. And outside the tent was a young woman digging about the shed, making a bed for plants. I stared at a pair of trunks flapping in the wind; getting a photo of what it was hiding would be as easy as getting pregnant.

We had just finished felting The Taj's roof, and Helen, weak now with laughter, was tidying up our tools, when Mum texted to see if I had anything yet. When I explained about the tent she swore. Since Mum's discovered speech-to-text on her phone her messages have turned into long-winded blogs with the odd predictive mistake.

Ms Frasier says you're to commando sneak, she sent – that meant crawling on my stomach, I assumed.

It's been raining, the ground is a mud slide, I texted back.

Snooping is not weather dependent, it is anything but, you must commit, overcome and get some friggin' pictures for our operations room. How can we operate with no pictures?

I swore at that.

Here was I with impending sterility, feet that a bird of prey would be ashamed of, a smear test on the horizon, and she who called herself my mother wanted me to crawl like a snake under a pile of washing camouflaging a bonsai Red Riding Hood.

What would it take for her to care?

Incontinence?

Steven called me dramatic when I messaged him, but then texting to him is a one-two maximum worded affair, especially when it comes to my mother.

Ignore xxx, he texted, followed by a heart.

My phone pinged again: Ms-friggin'-Frasier, claiming my mother was frantic.

She obviously hadn't worked out the speaking text. *I am trying to work here,* I sent back. Then Helen grabbed my phone off me.

"Let's go inside," she said. "We've finished here for the day and I can smell The Chef's cooking."

Chapter Thirty-Five

RESTORATION

I'd shag you if I was on that side of the fence, batted from the other side

Sheryl

I followed Helen into The Taj, where a grim-faced Neff was making coffee for Hia, The Roadworks Man and a tiny woman they introduced as Ewa. Hia was talking about her conference: Ayurvedic medicine and yoga, and so sending Neff into a series of tuts. She started doing her best to out-talk Hia with her standard lecture on pelvic exercises and dry underwear but she was failing miserably. Even The Roadworks Man had heard it all before and as he said, "If such things did work, more women would be doing them."

Tenzam was looking chipper, which seemed to rile Neff even more. Then when Ewa picked up a menu and began to talk of what to order, Neff nearly threw a hairy fit.

"Hurry up, then," she snapped, sniffing like there was a gas leak. "We haven't got all day."

"She's having what we're having," said The Roadworks Man.

"Oh," muttered Neff.

I plonked onto a seat with a sigh. Hia caught my eye with a look that reminded me of my mother. "You finished?" she said.

"Another day should do it." Helen took the seat beside me.

"Another day?" Hia huffed.

Tenzam began to explain how things were different in Scotland and when Hia pulled a "really" face, he left for the kitchen.

"I went out with a builder once," said Ewa. "*Tomorrow* was his favourite word and tomorrow never came."

"Yes, well, Sheryl and Helen are different," Neff told her.

"His word was as reliable as the friggin' trains," said Ewa.

"When Sheryl and Helen say tomorrow, *they* mean it," insisted Neff.

"Really?" said Ewa. She looked closely at my round arms, pressing her fingers into the muscle, which was quite painful considering how tiny her fingers were. She laughed. "You have the arms of a man."

"Not when she's belly dancing," said Neff. "Sheryl's my best student, dances like a goddess."

Ewa eyed me some more. "I'd love to see that."

My face began to burn.

"You're so muscular," she told me.

"Muscular?" I tried to joke. "I'd call it fat."

Tenzam shouted Neff to the kitchen at that point, and Neff, with a weird look at Ewa, disappeared.

Ewa, her eyes on me, didn't seem to notice Neff at all and I was beginning to feel uncomfortable. Ewa was looking at me in a way that made me feel naked, like she could see through my clothes to what was underneath and my underneath was as co-ordinated as The Bag Lady's tent.

"Hot flush?" said Ewa. "Too much sugar. You need tofu."

"That's what my husband says," I muttered, wishing she would stop giving me the eye.

"Or perhaps some nutmeg, or turmeric. There are plenty of herbs," Hia chipped in.

"He says that too."

"What do men know?" Ewa shrugged.

"I could write you a list," said Hia.

"He's already done that – in a friggin' notebook," I said.

"Her husband is a librarian," Helen said to Ewa.

"Pff, men," said Ewa. "My "husband" lives on the other side of Scotland on a fish farm."

Thank god, I thought, *she has a husband.*

"Catching his attention is like trying to catch a trout without a fly, unless we're in bed." She looked at my breasts. "Sometimes I think I would be better off with a woman."

"Here, enough of that talk," muttered The Roadworks Man. "I'm about to eat."

Oh god maybe she's a swinger, I thought.

"Your mum just texted." Neff stood at the doorway and looked at me.

"Mum? To you?"

"Yes, she said you were avoiding her," said Neff, with another weird look at Ewa.

I looked at my phone; the battery had died.

"She said something about a photo."

When I explained, The Roadworks Man laughed so hard his eyes welled up.

"I'll help you get the photo," said Ewa. "I've been in that garden all afternoon and I know the very place to get down on your stomach."

Helen caught my eye.

'I was thinking more about a diversion," I looked from Neff to Helen, "at the Red Cross shop."

"I'll do it," Neff offered.

I knew she would; Neff has a thing for that Red Cross shop, she can't walk past it without going in, especially when "She-who-lives-to-Moan (as Neff called her) is there. Neff just loves to wind her up.

"Come on, then," said Ewa, almost grabbing my hand to haul me out.

I could swear Helen was stifling a laugh as we left, but within seconds Ewa was talking about sex and me in the same sentence. At first I thought it was some weird joke until I did get onto my stomach to crawl.

"I'd shag you if you were on the other side of the fence," Ewa said. "Ride you into the sunset."

I was manoeuvring myself under a large wet pair of overalls at the time, realising that "She-who-would-shag-me" (as Neff would definitely call her) was behind, dangerously close to what she called my bite-able rear.

She started talking about the other side of the fence when we walked out of The Taj, talking like I would eventually give in, let her have her wicked way with me. She was more suggestive than a drunk married man, worse than even my ex, Martin, who liked to put it about like fly spray. But no – she wasn't suggestive at all, she was as open as a prostitute on a corner shouting, "A fiver for a blow job."

"I don't swing that way,' I grunted – yet again.

She crawled up beside me. "Why not climb over the fence, just once – for a taste."

"Does your husband know about you and the whole other side of the fence thing," I said, inching away from her.

"He loves it," she gushed. "He's the sort who wants to watch, or join in." She crawled closer. "You fancy a trip to Aberdeen?"

I shoved her away. "No."

"Have you *ever* tried the forbidden apple?"

I moved on. "You calling it an apple now?"

"I am sure one bite would be enough," she drawled.

"I am happily married," I said. "And very satisfied."

"You looked pissed off to me," she said. "That was the first thing I noticed about you..."

I stopped, turned to her. "You don't know my mother."

"...all tight and tense like you're needing a good seeing to," she went on, ignoring me. "Here let me loosen those knots in your neck."

"My neck is fine."

"No, it's not, you're tense. Here, let me."

I pushed her hand away. "Don't touch. How can I crawl when you're playing Pattie Cake on it?"

"I wouldn't call it Pattie cake, darl." She returned her hand. "You're all tight and hard." She moved her hand lower. "Here, by the kidneys."

I pushed her hand away again. "Leave my kidneys alone."

"Five minutes with me and you'd be as floppy as a piece of spaghet-ti," she said. "I do Hawaiian massage."

"You're the last person I want to be floppy with," I said. "Besides, I've a smear test tomorrow."

"You're so funny. I bet you laugh your head off when you come."

My face burned a bright red; I had almost forgotten why I was there. I had gone from embarrassed and intimidated to pissed off quicker than it took to suck a chocolate button and still she had an answer for everything.

We got to the tent and stopped inside. I jumped to my feet. She followed with a bigger jump and a fake stumble, pressing herself onto me to balance.

"I knew it," she said. "Bet you're as noisy as a horse...as rampant as..." She stopped.

We looked around.

The tent covered a large section of grass, which now had spiral paths to something large and covered in yet another sheet.

"Just how paranoid can a woman be?" muttered Ewa.

I nodded.

"I mean what is so friggin' precious it needs another sheet?"

We lifted the sheet...and stared...

There was not a stuffed turkey or a chipolata in sight. Just a work of art.

A sculpture so perfect it would give Michelangelo's David a run for its money; so scary, it'd have children screaming; so life-like it almost moved; and so magnificent it stopped Ewa and her sex talk.

Two bonsais were twisted into a Red Riding Hood and her grandmother, so realistic they not only had eyelashes but looked about to blink with terror. And towering over them, like he was about to swallow them whole was a giant wolf. The wolf had been clipped from a hedge, with a snarling jaw wide enough to swallow a truck and a snake-like tongue stretched out in a lizard curl. It was inches from Red Riding hood's hood, alluding to drool.

I stared at the mistletoe bow pinned on Red Riding hood's hood – the only thing faintly festive about it. "We haven't a chance," I muttered.

"Absolutely none," whispered Ewa.

Chapter Thirty-Six

RED CROSS SHOP

The art of winning is knowing when to give up

Neff

I was loitering by the second-hand underwear rack in the Red Cross shop, doing my best to divert, when I realised there was no need.

Not that I would ever buy second-hand underwear. I'd rather go commando, swing braless, Germaine Greer style, than slip on someone else's smalls, and She-who-lives-to-Moan knew it, but she wasn't even looking at me. She was training up an apprentice called Jean and was completely full of it. By the till was a manual and she, glasses around her neck, pen in her hand, was making a big thing of flicking through the pages, muttering about health and safety.

I was beginning to feel a little surplus to requirements, wondering if I should head back to the restaurant, when Jean disappeared, with a slam of the door. I hovered but she was soon back, clutching two roll and sausages from the chippy. She slapped the rolls onto the counter with a, "You'll never guess what I just saw."

She-who-lives-to-Moan didn't look up. "You'll need to eat that outside or at least near the back door," she said.

I was about to jump in, try a bit of diverting when–

"They had a right old ding-dong in the street," said Jean.

"Those two are always fighting," muttered She-who-lives-to-Moan. She peered at her roll. "Perhaps we can eat in here, just the once."

Phew, I thought.

"But this time it was different," said Jean.

She-who-lives-to-Moan pulled out a sauce sachet. "A fight's a fight with them two." She slid the sauce sachet between her teeth and began to tug.

"No. This time it *was* different..." Jean paused. "...sustainable fish."

She-who-lives-to-Moan stopped tearing the sachet. "No?"

Jean pulled out a pair of scissors and grabbed She-who-lives-to-Moan's sauce sachet. "I'm telling you, it was some scene." She cut the sachet with a decisive snip.

"Blood all over the Captain Birdseye's Santa.

Jean squished sauce onto she-who-lives-to-Moan's roll and pressed it together. "Jason was shouting when I walked in."

"He's deaf," She-who-lives-to-Moan pointed out, "he always shouts."

"I mean red-faced shouting." Jean handed the roll over and then took a bite from her own. She swallowed, and with a gulp launched into a monologue that had me forgetting about the tent, Sheryl and that friggin' Ewa. "Jason appeared right in the middle of the high school chip butty queue."

"Typical." She-who-lives-to-Moan snorted.

"He pushed his way through, yelling about fishing trawlers destroying the ocean."

"That old chestnut," scoffed She-who-lives-to-Moan.

"Then he started calling Captain Birdseye the prince of darkness, the destroyer of the ozone."

"You're joking," said She-who-lives-to-Moan, her roll inches from her lips.

"Gordon said he was just trying to make a living, and didn't give a flying fuck when his fish came from and do you know what Jason said?"

She-who-lives-to-Moan shook her eager head.

"He said, "You will when there's bugger all to batter." So glad I don't eat fish." Jean took another bite, then swallowed. "Gordon got angry and told him to fuck off. He said the price of Jason's haddock was so high he may as well try and sell caviar. Jason told Gordon not to be ridiculous, which riled Gordon even more. He started to jostle Jason out of the chippy, yelling, "You can shove your gold-plated haddock". Gordon pushed Jason so hard he shot out of the door like a cannon ball landing smack bang into Captain Birdseye. Fishing tackle flew across the road, and Jason started to yell about Gordon stealing his...well...his tackles. That sent the students into hysterics." Jean stopped to peer at the door at the back.

She-who-lives-to-Moan followed her gaze.

I, in an engrossed panic, grabbed a way-too-small bra and shouted, "What do you think if this."

She-who-lives-to-Moan, clearly catching sight of something "afoot" in the green ignored me. "Is that the Polish carer," she asked.

"She's not Polish," Jean said.

"The Roadworks Man says she is."

I pulled the bra across my chest and looked at myself in the mirror. "What do you think?"

"Pff him," said Jean. "How many time does that guy have to get things wrong before you stop listening?

"Sounds Polish," muttered She-who-lives-to-Moan.

I waved the bra about the counter – right under their noses. "A smaller size?"

"No, she doesn't," said Jean. "She's just got a weird accent from travelling all the time."

"I thought she was married." said She-who-lives-to Moan.

"She's married?" I blurted out.

"And that's weird, too," Jean agreed. "She tried it on with my sister."

That stopped me again. "Your sister? Why would she do a thing like that?"

"Lesbian," mouthed Jean.

"In Lochgilphead!" said She-who-lives-to-Moan. It took a while for her to recover from such a revelation, a while, along with a roll and sausage, a packet of crips, two cappuccinos and several sachets of sauce.

Jean played out the attempted seduction of her sister with more gusto than an amateur dramatic drama, claiming, "*She* would flirt with her own shadow."

She-who-lives-to-Moan was all ears, her mouth gaping like a stunned fish.

"Apparently she just doesn't give up." Jean licked her fingers. "And she has the language of a porn star."

"What language does a porn star use?" said She-who-lives-to-Moan." *As if she had no idea.*

"Sort of "Fifty Shades of Grey," said Jean, "with more swearing."

We stared at the garden as Sheryl crawled from the tent, stood up, and adjusted herself. Ewa followed her and stood close, made as if to talk.

"I thought Sheryl was happily married," observed Jean.

Sheryl marched off. Ewa followed.

"She still is by the look of things," I said. I stood by the toiletries section, idling over what had happened to the Lily-of-the-valley soap. To say I felt relieved was like saying The Roadworks Man had no idea of the truth. I picked up a Dove gift pack and pondered a mini celebration. Losing Tenzam to Ewa, it seemed, was as possible as Beatrice cartwheeling across Lochgilphead green. I opened the Dove box and, ignoring She-who-lives-to-Moan's glare, sniffed.

My mobile rang.

Tenzam: high school students were mobbing The Taj, due to the police closing the chippy. There was a rush on pakoras and chips. "Quick," he said. "I can't pack fast enough."

"I've got to go," I said. I slapped the gift set on the counter with dramatic, "Emergency at The Taj."

"The Taj?" Jean turned to She-who-lives-to-Moan. "Love that Tenzam, such a nice young man."

"He's not that young," I said. "He's older than he looks."

"What he needs is a nice young girl," Jean carried on, "someone he can have kids with."

"Not everyone wants kids," I observed.

"He does. He loves kids, you should see him with my daughter's two." Joan stopped. "Maybe I could ask her, she's got a few single friends."

"Never match-make," She-who-lives-to-Moan told her, while sliding my Dove gift set into a bag.

"Hear, hear," I said.

"Besides. he's probably got someone back in India lined up."

"It's Bangladesh," I corrected her.

Silence.

"He is from Bangladesh, not India and he doesn't have anyone lined up. He's perfectly happy as he is."

The two women looked at me as if they'd just noticed I was there.

"I knew that," muttered Jean with a decisive jangle of my change.

Chapter Thirty-Seven

LEFTOVERS

One person's leftovers is another's caviar

Neff

The Taj was, indeed, heaving with high school students when I arrived back, and soon I was packing and taking money, too busy to say or do anything else. It took a half an hour to clear the queue, a half an hour during which Tenzam and I silently served, perfectly into tune with each other.

Working with him and The Chef was always easy, we seemed to get on without speaking. Tenzam brushed past me several times, like he always did, sending my heart into a flutter. I had never noticed before how closely we worked, yet now it was all I could think about. It was like being a schoolgirl again, bursting into stupid giggles over nothing.

Tenzam, sliding the till shut, smiled at me. "Thank you, Neff."

The last student had left, and we started clearing the devastation of queueing teenagers, when Sheryl and Ewa appeared, talking of photos.

"Mission accomplished," said Ewa. She followed it up with an equally unfunny, "Been busy?"

I laughed – wholeheartedly, a full head back laugh – I was as high as a helium balloon. Sheryl and Ewa looked at me like I had two heads, while Hia called Tenzam from the kitchen, then produced two mugs of tea. She handed one to Tenzam, talking in their language.

The Chef and Tenzam often talked in their language and it never bothered me. I had even picked up a few words, strung the odd completely wrong sentence together, which always got a laugh, but with Hia it was different. They were very close and when she talked to him it was like I wasn't there. It seemed they had things to discuss which had nothing to do with me. I watched the two of them head into the kitchen, talking with The Chef like they were solving some sort of world food crisis.

I felt as left out as a mistress on Christmas Day.

"The family want him to help run their restaurant in Glasgow, while a cousin comes here," said Ewa.

My heart sank like a brick in quicksand.

"How do you know?" asked Sheryl.

"The Roadworks Man," said Ewa.

"Pff, him." Sheryl gave me a soft look. "Wasn't him who thought Hia was his wife."

That night I ate nothing. My fridge was full of leftovers: chicken on its last legs, cheese a bit on the hard side, ham curling at the edges, but I couldn't face any of it. I was too down, too miserable. Instead, I decided to feed what was left of the chicken to The Daughter of Ramses Two – as The Bag Lady had gone all veggie and I was as hungry as a prisoner heading for the electric chair, the cat bowl was the only place for it.

I sloped into the kitchen full of self-pity and threw open the fridge. Silence.

Nothing. Not a meow, a purr, or the thud of her landing from the window.

I shut the fridge door. I stared at the spot where The Daughter of Ramses Two usually appeared. *Where was she?* That cat could hear the fridge open a mile away, over the rumbling of a truck, the roar of a lawn mower, the TV on full. Whenever I opened the fridge, The Daughter of Ramses Two was there, behind the door, and glaring at me with a full on I'm starving meow, when I shut it.

I opened the fridge again, rattled the door – and stopped. It was virtually empty, just a lone slice of soya ham. *Where was the chicken, my eggs, my cheese?* I shut the door again, pulled out the packet of cat biscuits and commenced rattling, which usually had her scurrying and skidding in.

Nothing.

I poured the biscuits into her dish and waited for her to appear, sniffing like she had never sniffed a cat biscuit before. She aways did that and then she'd walk away leaving the bowl untouched. The strange thing was the biscuits were always gone in the morning, like she snuck in and secretly ate them. In fact, I caught her once, chomping down on the biscuits late at night. I had woken with a "shit, did I lock the back door?" panic jolt (watching a Steven King film alone can do that to a woman), and crept into the kitchen catching her mid gulp, shamefaced as if she had been caught eating from my plate.

I walked to the back door, shook the box of biscuits and called out – no easy feat with that name.

I waited, staring at the sunset, confused. The dusk light was playing shadows in my garden but I saw nothing, heard nothing, not a faint flicker of a fire, or a chuckle from Betty. Where the hell were they all?

I took the bowl of biscuits, un-sniffed and untouched, and slid a slice of soya ham on top. The chances of The Roadworks Man being right about anything were as probable as The Daughter of Rameses polishing off this soya slice, and yet his words stung. I was always the last to know, told nothing. I wasn't even an afterthought, I was invisible, yet I was expected to drop everything at a moment's notice, like their friggin' slave.

How stupid I was to think of us – me and Tenzam – together. It was not just that age difference but everything. It had taken me a while to get the hang of The Taj, and Tenzam's ways, and even though I had, I was still an outsider. We were so different; eating curry with my hands wasn't even the tip of the iceberg when it came to being one of them.

Tenzam had a large family; I had a cat and The Bag Lady. He was a Muslim and I had a buddha in the garden. And don't get me started on the language. I mean, I struggled to remember road directions, let alone words from another country. I would never be fluent in Bangla, let alone enjoy a joke and all the other things Tenzam and his sister shared.

I thought about my mother, how broken she was when the Prince left, and never came back, how scared I was when Rodger left me. Being single was better than going through all that again.

I looked at the soya slice untouched and beginning to curled at the edges. I took the dish to the back door and peered into the garden again. *Where the hell was that cat?* I flicked on the outside light.

"Daughter of Rameses Two," I shouted.

The Bag Lady appeared, inches from my face, as if in a ghost film.

'Jesus!" I screamed.

"Shit!" she yelled.

We stopped, stared at each other.

"I thought you were still at work," she puffed.

"Finished early. What–" The Bag Lady had the look of someone waiting for the results of a cancer scan, which had me in a panic. Her looking concerned was as rare as her looking for the Hoover.

"What's up?" I said.

Before she could reply, Betty charged up, also puffing. "The fence is sorted..." she gasped, then stopped. "Neff. Shit."

I looked over her shoulder; my fence was held up by a series of poles and was not looking too solid.

"What's going on?" I asked again.

Chapter Thirty-Eight

JUMP

Sometimes the only thing to do is close your eyes and jump

Neff

According to Betty, Go Boy had been barking "full swing" all afternoon, on account of being left on his own for most of the day. The Bag Lady got so fed up she flung the remains of a cottage pie at him, forgetting that the pie, like her, was vegetarian. Go Boy took one sniff and hurled himself at the fence. With no Jason to shout, 'That'll do' or slap him silly, Go Boy went from hurling, to launching, to catapulting and finally to head-butting like a goat.

"Years of newspaper slapping, of pent up yearning to jump the fence, raged in his loins," said Betty.

"He head-butted the fence," The Bag Lady corrected her.

"Demolished it like a tornado of testosterone," said Betty.

"I wouldn't say demolished, exactly," said The Bag Lady.

"That fence went down like a deck of cards, a tower of dominoes," Betty insisted. "One shudder and he couldn't stop. He was like a drug addict at a chemist, a thief by a safe, an alcoholic at a bar with the booze locked away–"

"I get the picture," I said.

"He ran about the garden like a crazed Zulu warrior," she added.

"And the only way we could get close to that dog to tie him up was to throw food at him," The Bag Lady told me.

"From your fridge." Betty now re-enacted the scene...

For a moment I forgot my cat, Tenzam, even the destruction of my fence, as Betty put on a Bruce Lee fight performance.

"Rodger fixed the fence,' interrupted The Bag Lady, with a "that's enough" look at Betty.

"My Rodger? How did you get him to do that?"

"Shifty," said Betty a little puffed. "Despite what he says, he likes helping his mum."

"What about The Daughter of Ramses Two," I said. "Was she anywhere near this act of pent up, groin-raging, mass destruction."

"I saw a ball of fur dart across the garden into the drive," said Betty. 'And we've haven't seen her since."

———

Sheryl

That night I jumped on Steven and rode him like it was our honeymoon. It was the sort of sex went on so long he slept late the next day, and when he finally woke he had the look of a love struck teenager. I told him about Ewa and he went all "Fifty Shades of Grey" and wanted to do it again.

I guess it was all Ewa's dirty talk under the tent that aroused feelings in me I had forgotten. It's not that I wanted to head up to Aberdeen and put on a show for her husband, but there was something about her that triggered an angry lust in me.

Steven was pretty speechless. With a kiss on his head, I left him pouring over a Hawaiian massage website

"Did you know it's done with no clothes on?" he said. "Just a loincloth."

I turned back to see his face like a child's at Christmas time. "I wonder where I can order one?"

Chapter Thirty-Nine

THE SMEAR TEST

Performing does not always require a stage

Sheryl

I was sitting, preened for a smear test, in the GP's waiting room. And like the rest of them waiting, I was masked, over-egging my smile to what I thought were familiar faces.

The GP and hospital are in one building with a waiting room that had the remains of social distance restrictions laid out, the acoustics of an opera house, and a canteen with machine coffee, pre-made sandwiches and a frustrated chef/manager.

I had forgotten about the Red Cross shop's masterpiece, and how I was going to break the news to Mum; too busy enjoying the memory of last night. I felt so happy, so lust struck I could burst into song, even the "how to wash your hands" video at the GP's made me chuckle.

It had been a long time since I had seen Steven that happy. The last time I remember him looking so elated was when Baby Bea was born – holding her, he was a picture of joy, while I was getting stitched up like a sock with a hole. I thought I'd never have sex again, that the hedgehog feeling between my legs would never heal.

Now I couldn't wait to do it again. I began to re-tell and exaggerate the whole Ewa story in my mind, expanding it, rehearsing it for Steven. I had just moved on to loincloths when Ms Frasier appeared with a, "There you are. I've been looking for you everywhere."

She plonked herself beside me and started to talk of the dangers of being alone and of Go Boy. Her monologues normally had me shrinking with embarrassment but today, as her Australian twang echoed around the waiting room, I listened with amusement.

"That dog had the fence down in minutes and was circling the yard like a caged lion. It took a whole chicken, a side of bacon and several cheeses to get near enough to him to tie him up. That's what being alone can do to a dog. I felt for it, I can tell you. I spend way too much time on my own – enough to talk to spiders," she said. "I crave company like a coke addict craves coke."

The elderly gent next to me leaned across to look at Ms Frasier. He was sitting with his daughter, gasping over his Zimmer frame like he was on his last legs, until she'd got going. He listened intently.

"A trapped audience has me as excited as that dog," she said. "Sparking off a spin of steamy jokes and one-liners, the sort a parent embarrasses their children with."

The elderly gent eyed her with a twinkle.

Ms Frasier paused and whispered to me, "I have a joke for every occasion."

The elderly gent chuckled, while I began to wonder where loin-cloths were sold and *were they disposable?*

"I find sex jokes work best on the NHS," Ms Frasier said directly to the elderly gent.

"Me too," he muttered, ignoring his daughter's, "Shh."

"Anyone who listens to me is fair game for a routine," said Ms Frasier. "I'm a slut when it comes to getting a laugh. Menopause can do that to a woman."

I laughed out loud, stopping Ms Frasier in her tracks.

The elderly gent took his chance, sliding into the silence with a banter of gossip and double entendres, silencing Ms Frasier. She had finally met her match, and even when he, mid wink, moved seamlessly onto the Garden Competition and how it had "ripped open decades of rivalry between Jason the fishmonger and Gordon who runs the chippy", she said nothing.

We were listening to an expert, a man who had spent his whole life embarrassing his family with jokes that should be heard only once – I could tell by the look on his daughter's face. And despite her trying to keep him in line, the old man continued filling the waiting room with his voice:

"There I was waiting for my cod and chips, when Jason charged in, demanding the return of his lobster pots and tackle."

His daughter blushed. I laughed. Ms Frasier, out-talked and out-joked didn't seem to mind, she was smiling.

"Gordon, brandishing a fish slice shouted, "My garden is friggin' Kosher", sparking off a row..."

"Dad," hissed his daughter, "don't exaggerate."

"...A row involving flying batter, mayonnaise sachets and the skidding of the fish monger."

How much of it was true I had no idea but it was making not only me but Ms Frasier laugh out loud.

"Tell me more." She chuckled. Then, "I've heard the Red Cross shop is the real contender," she added – silencing the waiting room.

Everyone stared, including the canteen manager mid coffee machine cleaning; she shut the machine with a slam and a stare.

"Pff. I seen their so-called garden and it has as much to do with Christmas as Ramadan."

"Dad, please don't be offensive." The daughter nodded at the Canteen manager. "She pals with the Red Cross manager." She turned to the woman. "He'll be on about the war next." She feigned a laugh.

"I was never in the war," said the elderly gent.

"Yes, but you still talk about it," his daughter hissed.

He huffed. "That garden is as much a garden as I'm a batsman."

The practice nurse leant close to my ear, stopping the elderly gent mid flow (on one of his favourite subjects according to his daughter). "Would you mind awfully if a student practices on you?"

"Student?" The old man heard her. "No students coming near my bits and pieces, they're in enough trouble as it is."

"She wasn't talking to you..." The daughter's face was beetroot red.

But the nurse smiled at him.

"Can't even get a good night's sleep thanks to my friggin' prostate and you want some whippersnapper to have a rummage?"

He peered at me over his mask and winked. "You have a prostate too?"

Ms Frasier chuckled as the nurse led me down the corridor, asking me again if it was all right for a student to "have a go?"

Mind? I thought, *My fanny's just had the seeing to of a life time, she's as ready as she'll ever be.* Then with no warning it came out...an orgasm-tinted joke of bad taste.

"My fanny's had more viewings than a house auction, what's one more?" I said cheerfully.

The nurse, with a crisp rustle of her plastic apron, said nothing.

I couldn't help myself. "My fanny has seen more strangers than the London Tube."

The nurse opened the door to a slip of a girl, who didn't look old enough to order a pint let alone be a student doctor. I caught the student's eye and she smiled.

"...Not that there have been many complaints."

She definitely laughed.

I toyed with the idea of cracking the standard, "At my age, you got to take what you can get" joke but decided against it. It didn't really fit with the "I've been around the block so many times I've lost count" theme and as I have heard Ms Frasier say many times it's best to coordinate jokes: warm up with one theme, build a narrative of expectation, rather than throw them out randomly like an amateur fisherman. Especially in a clinical room with all the warmth of a morgue. That had the sort of cold atmosphere no amount of heating could destroy, and the sort of implements that usually had me sitting with my legs crossed. Not today...I was feeling too happy.

The nurse told me to strip, gesturing to the bed with a, "Make yourself comfortable," like the two went together. She and the underage student disappeared behind the curtain and I removed my bottom bits, and jumped onto the bed.

"The last time I did this for a stranger, I was pissed," I said.

Was that a laugh?

"And that wasn't yesterday."

They swished open the curtain. I positioned myself into the sort of pose that required a lot of deep breathing. "And this is where the cleaner comes in," I joked.

The youthful student slipped on her gloves with a condom-style flick, smeared gel over her larger-than-life implement then, with shaky hands, turned to the nurse with a "which bit" look. There was a certain amount of prodding and fumbling; enough to make me glad she wasn't male and I hadn't eaten gas-inducing cauliflower before I came.

As I left the examination room, comfortable in the knowledge that my libido, like my jokes was on the up, I bumped into the elderly gentleman and his daughter heading for the exit. She clutching his prescription and he strutting while holding his Zimmer in pointless way.

He caught my eye. "Curing the prostate is a piece of piss, according to the doctor."

"Dad, he didn't say that."

"May as well have." He stopped with a smile and turned to wave at Ms Frasier, who was also making her way along the corridor. "We're off to the chemist for a carry-out," he shouted.

"Pills, Dad."

"At my age, it's a carry-out."

He leaned toward me. "The days of a half bottle and a bit of how's your father are gone for me. Now it's pills, creams, and if I'd lucky a few hours kip."

"You sleep like a horse, Dad." The daughter shook her head.

I laughed.

"A carry-out for me is a tube of lubricant and a tub of denture cream," Ms Frasier shouted back.

He caught her eye. "Make the most of it, honey. One day it will be Senokot and a hot water bottle."

Ms Frasier, out ad-libbed yet again, laughed, as he with a wink muttered. "My work here is done."

I watched, safe in the knowledge that even a smear test could not wipe the grin from my face. I spied a menopause leaflet by the reception desk. I had seen it before, brought a couple home and cried over them. Not today. For the first time I didn't feel that stab in my stomach, the sadness was more bearable. The laughter had engulfed the sadness and every time I conjured the memory of last night, the hard edges of pain softened a little more.

Chapter Forty

ROAST POTATOES

Leftovers are best eaten standing

Sheryl

Steven was still in his 'Fifty Shades of Grey" mode when I arrived home that night – despite Baby Bea being full of a cold and looking grumpy.

"Let's get her to bed early," he said. "Then I will make you something nice. "

Baby Bee was out like a light without even a breastfeed, the cold had really knocked her for six, not to mention the Calpol. I tucked her in, flicked off the light and headed into the kitchen.

"In here," Steven yelled from our bedroom. "Your massage awaits.

———

Neff

The Bag Lady, Betty and I spent the whole day looking for The Daughter of Ramses Two and were mulling over a coffee in the kitchen when Ms Frasier appeared. She was full of her encounter with Mr Finlay whom she had apparently, "clicked with" at the GP's surgery.

"There I was trying to extract strategic garden data from Sheryl and the next thing I know Mr Finlay and I are 'cracking the banter' like ol' pros. I even met him in the chemist afterwards. He was joking about his takeaway and I was laughing—" She looked at us. "Something wrong?"

"It's The Daughter of Ramses Two," I said.

"We haven't seen her since yesterday," said The Bag Lady.

———

Sheryl

A few hours later and there I was, greased up like a spark plug sliding about the bed sheets, while Steven slept as deeply as Baby Bea in her cot.

I stared at our bedroom window enjoying that delicious feeling of unexpected sex. The sort that is five parts massage, and one part legs in the air, moaning. My back had been massaged with an inch of its life, my feet wrung out like a tea towel as Steven started soft then went for deep tissue manipulation. The effect left me, as Ewa would say, as limp as spaghetti.

I got up and went to the kitchen, opened the fridge, and pondered Steven's recent cooking. I was as hungry as a bear waking from hibernation and his cooking was as good as his massage. I found the plate of leftover roast potatoes and a jug of gravy, then slid the jug into the microwave and waited – making a mental to thank Ewa, before deciding she may take it the wrong way. I pulled the bubbling jug from the microwave and dipped in a potato. Steven made the best roast potatoes and always enough for leftovers. I bit into the crispy outside then went for another dip, another sprinkle of salt, wishing the whole world could feel as I did...well, at least the likes of Neff. Every bit of me oozed satisfaction, even the bit that yearned for a baby seemed quiet.

I looked out the window, watching the sun set, treasuring a moment of peace, until Steven appeared, looking dozy and disgruntled and talking into my phone.

"She's probably gone somewhere quiet to have her kittens. Cats do that." He looked at me and mouthed it "Neff."

Neff obviously continued to talk.

"Yes, well... I'll just hand you to Sheryl." Steven handed me my phone. "Her cat's missing."

I threw him a "thanks" glare. He lobbed back a "she's your friend" shrug.

The last thing I felt like doing was walking into a Neff drama. Neff has always been an over the top sort of person who sensationalised better than a tabloid paper. I could just imagine what she'd be like with this: over-egging the whole thing, while The Daughter of Ramses Two was probably curled up somewhere warm, and I was in the middle of a bliss moment, intent on savouring every second.

Down the phone, Neff inhaled a "woe is me" sniff.

"You ok?" I muttered.

"Yes...but I can't help thinking of her, somewhere cold." Sniff.

"It's a mild evening." I rolled my eyes at Steven.

He gave me a thumbs up, followed by an annoying "Baby Bea's out for the count" mime, to which I answered with a pissed off stare, my bliss now well and truly buggered.

"Maybe she's gone away somewhere quiet to give birth," I said, trying to sound vet-like. "I've heard they do that."

Neff blew her nose; I held the phone from my ear.

"You don't know that," she said. "You don't even know if she's had her babies."

"Kittens."

"She could be splattered across the road somewhere, flattened by a lorry..."

"Let's not let our imagination run away with us, shall we?" I said.

"...Her babies oozing out of her womb like egg yolks," said Neff, ending with a horse-like nose blow.

In the background, Baby Bea began her waking up burbles. I gestured to Steven to wait. He performed his famed "generic gesture", the sort that set my teeth on edge, that even after years of living together could, like the word "fuck", mean anything: I'm busy; don't disturb; your turn; "my mind has lit up with something fantastic, must get it down" or, his favourite, "I'm only available for emergences". And as I watched him head to his man cave under the stairs, I knew that right now it meant pretty much all of them. I heard a thump from

Baby Bea's room and watched as Steven pulled out his writer's chair –
deaf to the noise. He closed the screen behind him with a crisp click.

"I just can't stop thinking of her mashed across the tarmac somewhere," said Neff.

"Don't be so dramatic," I told her.

"If you can't be dramatic when a car has squashed your loved one,"
wailed Neff, "then when can you be?'

"She's probably somewhere, suckling her young...Isn't she, Steven?"
I yelled the last bit.

"How do you know?" said Neff.

Thump.

"She was like a daughter to me." Neff sniffed.

Thump!

"Steven?" I took the phone away from my ear and yelled. "What
did you put in Baby Bea's cot?"

"Cot?" echoed Neff.

"Just the usual..." Steven yelled back.

Thump.

"..Oh! And that toy laptop," he added.

"The toy laptop?" I said. "You put *that* in her cot?"

No answer.

"You know she'll just toss it at the wall." I huffed.

He said nothing.

'Typical," I muttered.

"Are you listening to me?" Neff shouted.

Baby Bea started to cry.

"Steven!" I yelled.

Baby Bea howled.

I headed into Baby Bea's bedroom, reassuring Neff that I was of
course listening and totally there for her, that she was not to worry...I
switched on Baby Bea's light, and to her pulled my best "I'm coming"
face. She glared at me.

"She's probably curled up somewhere warm," I said to Neff, putting
Baby Bee's toys back in her cot – except for the toy laptop.

She stretched out her arms for it and...I gave in, handing it to her.

"I can't help thinking of her innards drying out in the sun," Neff moaned.

"Positive thoughts, Neff," I said as Baby Bea hurled the toy laptop across the room, just missing the wall. Holding the phone between my ear and shoulder I lifted Baby Bea from her cot and balanced her on my hip as I tried to console Neff.

"The Bag Lady is out looking for her." Neff gulped. "With Betty and Ms Frasier. I should go as well, but every time I call her name I well up."

I went into the kitchen, flicked on the kettle, sat Baby Bea in her highchair, handed her a biscuit, put the phone in its stand and turned it on loud speaker – so friggin' loud it would disturb Steven.

Baby Bea tossed the biscuit onto the floor and held her arms up to me. I handed Baby Bea a cup of juice, she sniffed, ran her arm across her runny nose, sneezed, then began to grizzle.

"I should go out and look," Neff repeated, "but I just can't face the thought of seeing her all dead. Dead like," she started to whimper, "road kill."

I wiped Baby Bea's nose, wondering what had got into Neff, why she was being so wet – even for her.

"Maybe she'll turn up" I said. "With her babies, I mean kittens. Have you tried Facebook?"

"I haven't time for that."

"No, I mean put a post up about her missing, asking has anyone seen her?"

"Oh. I never thought of that," said Neff.

"Would you like me to do it?"

Neff whimpered a "Yes."

"Do you have a photo you can send me?"

Neff muttered, "I think so", through a nose blow.

I flicked through my iPad, quickly finding one of Neff's cats poised by the hot tub in her usual regal fashion. "Don't worry I've found a lovely picture of the Daughter of...er..." I wiped Baby Bee's runny nose "...the cat."

"Oh," said Neff.

Baby Bea pushed my hand away, tossed her mug at the floor and howled. I hit the Facebook app and began to type, marvelling at my ability to lifted Baby Bea on to my hip, at the same time. I posted the picture then began to hunt the cupboards as Baby Bea used my shoulder for a tissue.

"Where's the Calpol?" I yelled at Steven.

Baby Bea put her head on my shoulder and coughed.

I patted her head. I found the Calpol.

"Don't worry," I yelled at Steven. "I've found it, just you carry on, I'll deal with everything."

"You found my cat?" squealed Neff.

"No, the Calpol," I said sitting Baby Bea on the bench.

"Oh."

I opened the bottle, fed her a spoonful, then lifted her back on my hip. On the phone, I heard Ms Frasier walk into Neff's kitchen, The Bag Lady and Betty following.

"I'll put you on loud speaker," Neff said to me.

I told her there was no need, I could just hang up, that I was in the middle of something, but I may as well have pissed into a gale force wind expecting it not to blow back. Neff, with the sort of nose-blowing that would put you off your food, talked of mashed innards and squashed babies.

"Kittens!" yelled Betty.

"She'll be having them somewhere," said Ms Frasier. "In Australia it's somewhere cool, here it will be somewhere warm."

"That's what Sheryl says." Neff sobbed.

"Do want me to put it on Facebook for you? Do you have a photo?" said Ms Frasier.

"Sheryl's done it."

"Oh, can I see–" Ms Frasier stopped.

At the same time, Steven yelled, "Have you seen Facebook?"

"I thought you we're writing," I hissed in his direction.

"Jesus," muttered Ms Frasier. "Have you seen this?'

"Has someone found my Daughter of Rameses Two?" cried Neff.

"Shit!" said Ms Frasier.

"What!"

Then I saw it: a post on the Garden Project Facebook page.

The Led and Isobel had run off together.

Chapter Forty-One

RESIGNATION

Folk believe anything if it suits

Sheryl

The Lead, inspired by an inflated sense of importance and a love for all things royal – including the disgraced ex King George – had left a long winded post. A post which Ms Frasier, with a faint whiff of sarcasm, read out in her loud Australian drawl.

A few hours ago I discharged my last duty as the Chairman of the Community Garden Project and declare my allegiance to whoever takes over. You all know the reasons which impelled me to renounce my leadership but I want you to know that in making my mind up I did not forget your gardens or the trophy.

You must believe me when I tell you I have found it impossible to carry the heavy burden of judging gardens without the support of the woman I love. And I want you to know that the decision has been mine and mine alone – apart from hers, of course.

"Who cares?" snapped Neff.

"They could have waited till after the judging. I mean, everyone knew," said Ms Frasier.

"I didn't," said Betty.

"Me neither," agreed The Bag Lady.

"Who gives a toss?" said Neff.

"The secret was out the day they were caught in the library van," said Ms Frasier.

"Who gives a shit," said Neff.

"Shall I hang up?" I shouted at the phone.

"I am on the edge of a catastrophe and you're talking about the sex life of two people I hardly know?" Neff shouted louder. "How could you be so shallow?"

"Shallow? How very dare you" snapped Ms Frasier.

"I'll just say goodbye, then." I continued to yell.

"Absolutely thoughtless," said Neff.

"How about a nice cup of tea?" Betty sent Neff into a tirade.

"My cat could be smeared across the motorway, abducted by aliens and you're reading Facebook over a cup of tea?"

"I'll call back later" I bellowed, jolting Baby Bea.

The Bag Lady called Neff ridiculous; Ms Frasier called Neff sexually frustrated; then in hyper-huffing mode Neff called Ms Frasier sex-obsessed – at which point I figured Neff had forgotten about me and so I hung up.

I poured a coffee, placed something mushy in front of Baby Bea, and then noticed a pot on the stove.

"Steven? What's this on the cooker?" I called.

"What?"

"This pan full of...not sure..." I swirled it. "Is it porridge?"

Steven appeared, stood over the pot and sniffed it. "Looks like one of your mother's pots."

I stared at the mush Steven disowned, wondering about putting it down the sink, when Mum phoned.

She was surprisingly philosophical about the whole Facebook post, which by now had more comments than an Elon Musk twitter. She even talked of leaving a comment which she never does, but as she said, such a post was "begging for a smart arse comment."

"I mean, honestly, who does he think he is? The next in line for the throne?"

Steven mouthed "Beatrice?"

I nodded.

Steven, with a sigh, took over the feeding of Baby Bea.

"I thought you'd be cheesed off," I said to Mum.

"Not really," she replied. "Everyone knew they were having an affair."

"I didn't," I muttered.

"Once they were caught behind the library it was all over Lochgilp-head and beyond."

"Not this far out."

Steven, playing aeroplanes with a spoon of Baby Bee's food, winked at her. She chuckled, devouring the spoon full of food.

"Ms Frasier says they were fed up with the looks and comments and made a run for it," said Mum.

"Ms Frasier? When did you see her?"

"This afternoon, near Neff's house, pinned to the gate by that dog from next door."

"Go Boy had her pinned?"

Steven stopped mid aeroplane spoon two; Baby Bea grabbed his hand.

"Yes. Looking terrified," said Mum. "There she was, her back against the gate with this bear of a dog, paws on her chest, breathing right into her face, so close she was covered in spit."

"She ok?" I said.

"He wasn't growling or anything, just panting, spraying drool like a sprinkler. George stopped the car, and before he could shout, "You ok?" she turns to us and yells, "You got any chicken?" like I carry around chicken in a car."

"But she *is* ok, isn't she?"

Steven with a quizzing look at me served another spoon to Baby Bea; she laughed.

I turned my phone back to speaker mode.

"Then Tenzam appears and saves the day with a pakora."

"Pakora? What's he doing with a pakora?"

"He was delivering a few doors down."

"Does that man ever stop working?" Steven mouthed playfully at our daughter.

"He hurled the pakora at the dog," Mum went on. "Setting Ms

Frasier free to talk for Britain and so she did." Mum sighed. "I wonder who will do the judging now?"

"Don't know, Mum. I'm sure Ms Frasier has it all under control..."

"Not that I'm bothered. Went off the idea once I saw those Red Cross photos. They've got the trophy in the bag," said Mum with a much longer sigh. "Ms Frasier told Tenzam about Neff's cat."

"The Daughter of Rameses Two," I said.

"Stupid name, "Mum huffed. "I mean, who calls a cat that?"

I turned to Steven and mouthed, "This from a woman who calls her cat Puss."

He chuckled.

"He seemed genuinely moved," said Mum.

"That's just the way he looks," I muttered.

"No seriously, he said he thought he'd seen something – a cat by the loch near an overturned boat."

Steven, scraping the last of the food from the bowl like there was still plenty of food left, pulled a face at Baby Bea. She laughed.

"Have you got your phone on speaker?" asked Mum.

"Baby Bea likes to hear your voice," I said with a shrug at Steven.

"Hi, Baby Bea, you eat up all your food and just ignore daddy's stupid aeroplane spoons."

"Baby Bea loves my aeroplane spoons," said Steven, washing her bowl. He grabbed the pot of mush from the stove.

"Maybe I should tell Neff," I said. "She has been way over the top, don't know what's got into her."

"George says it's Tenzam leaving. You know she's got a thing for him."

"Tenzam's leaving?" I looked at Steven. "He's not leaving. Neff would be the first to know."

"The Roadworks Man says he is."

"Pff. The Roadworks Man? You don't want to listen to him," I said.

"He just makes stuff up," called Steven.

"Fake news personified," I added.

There was a pause.

"Oh, by the way, I left some food for the birds," said Mum.

Steven, poised by the bin and about to empty the pot, stopped. "Oh, when?"

"A while ago but...you...sounded er...busy, so I just left it on the stove."

Steven looked at me. "She was here?" he mouthed

I nodded.

"Ok," I managed. "Thanks, Mum." I made to hang up.

"Oh, and Sheryl?"

"What, Mum?"

"Don't worry – about the pot, I mean. Just bring it around the next time you're passing."

"Ok."

"...On seconds thoughts, just keep it."

That night as Steven toyed over the pot of bird food, wondering if composting was too good for it, I made to put Baby Bea to bed. She was grizzling from her cold and refused any breast milk.

Steven appeared with Calpol. I looked at him. "Why don't you put her down" I said.

"What about her feed?"

"She doesn't want any. Maybe it's time I stopped."

Chapter Forty-Two

CAT BISCUITS

A glare speaks volumes

Neff

I had just spent the last hour receiving the glaring of a lifetime from my three friends.

I'd behaved pretty badly and had a dreadful row with them about my cat. The Bag Lady called me passive aggressive, Ms Frasier accuse me of unresolved passion, and Betty made a cup of tea.

"How can you make tea at a time like this?" I said.

She didn't bat an eyelid. She, waiting for the kettle to boil, was staring at Facebook like it was more important than The Daughter of Ramses Two, and when I pointed that out they all turned on me, like I was ungrateful.

"We've been out in that drizzling rain while you've been in here, wailing uselessly," said one of them (can't remember which).

I pointed out I was in the kitchen, cat biscuits ready in case she turned up.

"I even went next door," said Ms Frasier.

"No one asked you to go over there," I said.

"Well, someone had to check and it wasn't going to be you." She stopped. "Thank God for Tenzam delivering food."

"Tenzam?"

"Yes, he saw me pinned to the gate and hurled a pakora at that dog."

"What was he doing there?" I said, trying to act casual.

"He was delivering to someone a few doors down."

"Oh. Her," I said. "She'd have her pakoras delivered on a gold plate if she could."

"I told Tenzam about your cat and he seemed genuinely moved."

"That's just the way he looks," muttered someone.

"No, seriously, he said he thought he'd seen a cat by the loch, but before I knew it he'd gone." Ms Frasier went on then about George and Beatrice stopping and leftover chicken, but I had stopped listening, all I could think of was Tenzam: *He cared enough to look for my Daughter of Rameses Two?*

The other women continued to talk about She-who-wanted-her-pakora-on-a-gold-plate, how she was so up herself she didn't hang out her washing but had her cleaner do it. I was staring out the window in a state of heart palpations, wondering what was Tenzam doing now?

It was then I heard frail meowing. *I thought it – he – was my imagination...*Until I turned to see Tenzam at my back door, and like a heroic fireman, he was carrying a rescued kitten. In a shoe box.

At first I didn't see her, The Daughter of Ramses Two. Then she looked up over the cardboard side, blinked at me, and with a silent meow returned to her kittens – all one, two, there...four of them.

I was speechless, my throat as tight as a support socking.

I could have said many things: "Thank you"; "You're my hero"; "Where were they?" but I didn't get a chance.

Those friggin' women: The Bag Lady, Betty and Ms Frasier, jumped in like schoolgirls. With a ridiculous amount of cooing they circled Tenzam like he was a pop idol and they wanted an autograph.

But Tenzam met my eyes and held them.

My heart raced, jumped, and skipped a beat. Everything stopped, like a freeze moment in a film, just him and me.

I smiled, he smiled back...Until his phone rang. He dived for his pocket, dropped the phone, picked it up, saw who was calling and clicked his tongue.

It was Hia.

"Your deliveries are getting cold," I heard her say.

He looked at me again. "Would you like me to bring you some pakoras when I have finished?"

The other women stopped mid cooing to listen.

"Or something ...um...spicier?"

Chapter Forty-Three

THE MORNING AFTER

An orgasm smooths the face way better than Botox, it's just harder to find

Neff

He was asleep beside me.

I stared at his long brown lashes, as he breathed heavily with the contentment of a sleeping baby.

Last night we had kissed for so long my lips looked like they were full of Botox.

He whispered in my ear, called me "Darling". His soft, warm hand soothed my skin, breaking down every reservation I had about being too old. He kissed every part of me, then rubbed my back into the sort of submission that had me aching for him to stop, to move to the next bit – the shagging bit.

It was without a doubt the best sex I had had for quite some time... Well, the only sex if I was honest. I'd not had any since The Change, but everything just sprung back into life. I wanted to shout, "God bless belly dancing." I wanted to run out into the street and proclaim, "Hip circles really do work." All that, *and* no fear of a baby. Plus the sort of teenage foreplay you did when trying to keep your virginity, the kind that goes on so long you're pulling him on top, screaming, "Just do it".

I was so taken aback I never got a chance to grab my KY. There she was, unopened, unused, beside my out of date Tampax, like an "I'm there if you need me" pal, a crutch in the corner when your leg has almost mended. But thanks to the sort of fondling I'd had only distant memories of, I'd forgotten all about her.

I slid out of bed to make a coffee, my back a little sore.

I stretched it, looking out of the window.

It was late in the evening, and The Bag Lady and Betty were watching the fire die down, while The Daughter of Ramses Two was warming herself, her kittens inside the teepee.

"Darling?" Tenzam whispered

I turned.

Tenzam pulled the sheets back with a lustful look and I slipped back into bed. The coffee could wait. And for my back, I was sure I had a tube of Deep Heat somewhere.

The next morning I woke to find him standing by the bed, getting dressed. I watched as he slid on his shirt.

The first time I saw Tenzam I was walking past The Taj and he was inside, folding napkins, intent on his task. He'd caught my eye and held it with a delicious smile, just like the one he gave me this morning.

I thought about marriage, headscarfs, and mosques. Would he expect me to come with him to one of those? I wondered if I should learn to cook curry. Would I meet his family, those in Glasgow − or maybe visit his country? Should I join a Bangla class online? I thought of holidays together, being a couple out for a meal, a walk, holding hands, sharing Christmas and Eid presents. Would he move in with me? Mend my shelves? Then I remembered he was rubbish with a hammer. I thought about us opening our own place, or maybe we could run a cat sanctuary? I thought about Mavis, Lumpy, Tenzam and me, all hanging out as couples do, socialising, having a few drinks, with Tenzam on the Diet Coke.

I eyed his butt as he slid on his trousers.

He turned to me, mid fly zipping. "I have to go."

"But it's ages before you open the restaurant," I said.

"It's Hia, she wants me to help her with something."

"What about breakfast? I could make you something?"

"It's okay." he said. "Hia has made breakfast."

I spent the day mulling over coffee and eating like a horse, singing while clearing up and humming as I sprung into the garden.

The Bag Lady, hanging out her socks on the pyramid, stopped to eye me. "You look happy" she said.

I smiled at her.

She smiled back. "Did he get away ok, then?"

I nodded a "yes", a luv on the tip of my tongue. I wanted to hug her small shoulders, wrap my arms about her long thin frame, pull her close and tell her what a pal she was, how much I loved having her in the garden. Instead I offered to dry her socks inside, as I always did and she, as always, laughed, with an, "I like the smell of fresh air about my feet." I told her I was working that evening, like she didn't know, and I could bring back something for her, anything she wanted, *as I usually did.* And she, *as always,* told me to bring enough for Betty.

Betty appeared from the tent as if she had been there all night. The Daughter of Ramses Two followed behind with a royal strut, as if *she* owned the place. I could hear her kittens meowing inside and was just about to enter for a pat when The Bag Lady said.

"Someone needs feeding,"

I followed Her Majesty back to the kitchen and while I filled up her bowl with the best of chicken, I began to fantasise about Tenzam *again*: him joining my morning rituals, sharing a coffee in the garden and something stronger by the bonfire at night, although what's stronger than Diet Coke, I don't know. I looked down at The Daughter of Ramses Two and imagined teaching him how to feed my cat, learning what she loves, how to cook the chicken just right.

When Hia leaves, I told myself, he will be his own man, have breakfast with me, and join me watching the cats feed and The Bag Lady hang out her socks. Perhaps...*Perhaps he could give up the restaurant, get a day job.*

The Bag Lady joined me in the kitchen, watched me pour another coffee. She pulled a mug from the sink and thrust it at me. "I remember it well" she said, "Lovemaking with a nice man."

I looked at her thin erect body, propped up by the sink, covered in tatty clothes, her grey hair pulled tight from her wrinkled face into a bun. Even with a photo of her youthful self fresh in my mind, her behaving badly with a man was hard to imagine. I handed her a coffee.

"We never imagine other people doing it, though, do we?" she said with a satisfied sip.

Chapter Forty-Four

TIKTOK

The film is never the same as a book except if you're a film lover and hate reading

Sheryl

A week after The Lead's abdication post on Facebook, Helen and I were taking a coffee break in the community centre and trying to ignore Lumpy's unhelpful suggestions.

The kitchen was to be turned into the library, while the library was to be turned into some sort of archive storage centre for the Council and Lumpy, it seemed, knew the best way to do such things. If Helen and I didn't need the work we would have turned it down. The thought of the library being reduced to a small room was not something either of us wanted to be a part of.

Steven, however, was resigned to the change.

Turns out McTaggart's pop-up library had been a ruse, sugarcoating to make the moving off the library into the community centre less offensive, and it had been planned for years. Not that even McTaggart himself was aware of it.

"You should take the job," said Steven. "If you don't someone else will. Besides, there's more chance of you two making a decent job of it than a big firm."

I thought people would be protesting, upset about the whole idea of it, and that it would be bad for our business. In the end no one batted an eyelid. The Lead's Facebook post had seen to that. Or so I thought.

We had just polished off our egg rolls and were on our second coffee, mulling over what in the kitchen to toss into the skip – or rather, was there anything we *shouldn't* – when Ms Frasier walked in, looking to fill her kettle.

She'd put a post on the Community Garden Project Facebook page; a new judge being needed, at least one, maybe two. And when the only (joint) reply she received was from Gordon and Jason, the committee held a meeting; the last thing they wanted, according to Ms Frasier, was a boxing match over the placing of gnomes.

Ms Frasier claimed the Facebook post was her idea. However, Janice said the Garden Committee was hopeful it they could find someone to tame Ms Frasier – and if it wasn't for Gordon and Jason's punch up they may have been contenders.

Ms Frasier took one look at us and said, "So it's true, they *are* shifting the library?"

"Afraid so." I said.

"After all your mother and I went through."

"Yes."

She sighed. "All those egg cartons, what a waste. Does Beatrice know?"

And before I could answer, let her know that Beatrice was more interested in Neff's ability to keep a young man happy in bed, Ms Frasier pulled out her phone and launched into a spiel about McTaggart's TikTok page. Ms Frasier on TikTok is as believable as, well, Mc Taggart on it, but there she was, flicking through his posts like an expert. I couldn't believe it; I was still getting to grips with Instagram.

"He set it up when he caught his wife and The Lead together," said Ms Frasier as she flicked.

"Everyone knows that." Lumpy was now pulling out his phone.

I didn't. Not that I let on.

Ms Frasier, as if reading my mind – or the confused look on my face – said, "He caught them in The Lead's greenhouse."

Did they ever use a bed, I wondered.

"*At it*, in full daylight," muttered Lumpy, immersed in his phone.

Helen pulled out *her* phone and also began to flick.

Next thing I knew I had three phone shoved in my face, putting me right off my cappuccino. Three phones in sync with a giffgaff video, a close-up of a deadly nightshade rhythmically pulsating to a high pitched, "Yes Yes Yes."

"Is that Isobel?" I said.

They pulled their phones away in unison and began to flick again.

"McTaggart read their messages on Isobel's phone," said Lumpy.

"While she was feeding the cat," said Ms Frasier.

"They have a cat?" I attempted a bit of diverting.

"Messages as dirty as compost under the fingernails," muttered Helen.

I didn't know what to say, apart from, "Have we not got something better to do than listen to a bit of how's your father on TikTok?" I may not care much for the McTaggarts or The Lead but having your mother hear you scream the sort of things that only the person you're having sex with should hear, is a humiliating experience. I felt sorry for the Led and Isobel.

I told Helen and co. I wasn't interested, that I'd rather have my innards stapled to my eyelids than listen to Isobel in ecstasy. Not that anyone heard. They were too busy talking about McTaggart, how he set a trap, told Isobel he was off to mow the grass for the bowling club.

"Next thing, he's climbing over The Lead's fence, spying on them in the greenhouse, recreating The Go Between."

"The Go Between?" I said.

"L.P. Hartley,' said Helen.

"Finlay says The Lead has a thing for L.P. Hartley," said Ms Frasier.

They shoved their phone in my face with another video. Not that you saw much, just The Lead's deadly nightshade shuddering to some sort of wolf cry. It was enough to put me off my egg roll – if I hadn't eaten it already. They removed their phones, continued to flick. I thought of Mum's pot on the stove...

I still hadn't faced her yet.

"It's not like they're the first to...you know...have sex in the garden," I said.

"The Lead's an ex English teacher," muttered Helen.

"I knew that," said Ms Frasier, which by the look of her face I seriously doubted.

"Oh?' said Lumpy.

"Of course, Finlay knows everything – he's got a cleaner."

We looked at her.

"Cleaners know everything – even more than me."

They shoved their phones in my face again – seedlings juddering to harmonious moaning.

"Pure genius," muttered Lumpy.

"Very Go Between," agreed Ms Frasier.

"Perhaps we should leave Isobel and her belladonna alone," I said.

Still nobody heard, still they were too busy flicking through their phones, searching for more god-awful videos.

"That Lead is a real prick," muttered Lumpy. "Neff says he never left a tip."

Ms Frasier looked up. "Neither does she."

Chapter Forty-Five

LUST AND FERTILITY

Lust knows no discomfort, every tree, car, couch is an opportunity

Neff

It was spring time, the best time for an affair. The bulbs burst forth, the world is like a musical and KY is half price at the chemist.

I was loved up and spaced out.

Every night Tenzam came to stay, filling my bed with the exotic aroma of Asian spices and aftershave. I was as addicted as an insomniac to sleeping pills. I was in lust, living in LaLa Land, gayly serving in The Taj like I was on Prozac, still high on the same spicy smells of the night before. A curry was no longer a curry to me; it was a lubricant, an aromatic reminder of Tenzam's dark eyes, his smooth hands and heady massages.

I couldn't remember a time when I'd experienced such tenderness, and I wanted more, I wanted to drown myself in such feelings. It was like when I first discovered belly dancing. I was addicted to the drums, the feel of the dance, watching, learning and, performing. Now I was addicted to Tenzam's warm brown skin, his smooth chest and nipples that seem to rise with just a touch. He made my bedroom feel like the Hilton, my body feel alive, and my woes were as forgotten as an old pair of slippers.

How a woman in her sixties could feel like this was a mystery. I thought all that lust stuff was behind me, memories to share by the fire, with The Bag Lady and Betty, but here I was making new memories, living on another planet – Planet Shagging – and my pals were cheering me on.

I worked in the restaurant when needed, usually at the weekend. And while Tenzam cashed up I'd head home, giddy with anticipation, sitting with The Bag Lady and Betty until he appeared with a smile and a carry-out. In the morning Tenzam stayed in bed while The Bag Lady and I did our morning ritual. Occasionally, he stirred as I appeared with tea for him – I'd learnt he was more a tea than a coffee person). He liked to hear about everything I did; even if he was busy on his phone, he always listened. Except, of course, when it was Hia. She was leaving at the end of the week and you would think they were planning a trek through the Sahara. I asked Hia to join us at The Bag Lady's bonfire for a good Scottish send-off but she shook her head with a pinched face, like I was asking her to come with me to the abattoir.

The Bag Lady said I was lust struck. "Make the most of it," she said. "One day he'll fart and it'll be downhill after that."

Betty told her not to be crude but I just laughed – Tenzam farting? As if.

———

Sheryl

It took a while for Mum to forgive Neff's wheelchair comment, not to mention Ms Frasier's "betrayal", as she called it. And it was all thanks to that minging pot full of bird food.

A month after The Daughter of Ramses Two was found, Neff appeared at my door positively glowing and armed with a bottle of malt and a box of chocolates. Baby Bea was in her highchair smashing her food with a spoon, while Steven was in his man cave, listening to the last of Neff's tapes.

It was one of those silent mornings between couples that follows a lack of sleep – care of Baby Bea. Steven said it was my turn to see to her and I said it was his and in the end we both got up. Steven put her in her highchair while I, in silence, mashed up a banana and ignored his, "She'll only spit it out." Which she did, very slowly and with a great deal of dribbling. Steven naturally made a meal of it, reminding me he was right way more times than necessary. In an "I hate it when you're right" silence, I made toast.

By the time Neff breezed in all happy and fresh, like some young thing in a fabric conditioner ad, Steven had spent several hours in his man cave, occasionally appearing to make his own coffee. I had changed Baby Bea several times, helped her scribble with a few crayons, picking them up when tossed across the room, and was now watching her destroy her lunch almost as efficiently as she had her breakfast.

Neff stood at the kitchen door, backlit by the sun and throwing a sort of Pope-like wave at Baby Bea. Baby Bea, having tossed her spoon to the wind, was engrossed in carrot stick thumping and didn't look up. I did, to see that Neff looked as radiant as royalty after having a baby. Her skin was glowing and smooth, and her purple hair lustrous and flowing like a really expensive wig. She was like a female Jesus, ready to bless; I almost expected the sunshine to follow her into the kitchen.

She strolled in, cheerfully yelled, 'Hiya," to Steven then cooed at Baby Bea while I, poised at the sink and wiping jam from crayons, wondered just how good in bed was Tenzam..? I shook myself; surely I just needed more sleep.

Neff began to talk of her creative juices firing on all cylinders – clearly stopping Steven in his tracks because I heard a muffled, *"What?"*

He was still working through the mountain of Neff recordings and to quote my knackered husband, "Getting nowhere fast." Neff's full-speed literary juices had already been recording like a maniac.

"Seems solitude is the last thing I need to create," she joked now. "A good old fashion seeing-to works better."

"If only," muttered Steven from his man cave.

"I'm going to bribe your mum." Neff gestured to her carrier bag. "I was wondering if this was her favourite?"

I peered into the bag, spied the Jura malt and wished it were me she was bribing. "I think you've nailed it," I said.

"The chocolates are for you," she added. "And Baby Bea, of course." Neff tweaked the baby's nose.

When I told Neff Mum was coming over, Neff was ecstatic, claiming kismet was on her side, *yet* again.

"Perfect timing," she cooed at Baby Bea, planting a kiss on her forehead. That had me stumped; Neff was as fond of children as she was line dancing.

Baby Bea, waving her carrot like a flag, giggled.

I looked up from the sink, mid mug-rinsing.

"Hardly Kismet," I said. "George phoned, Mum is wanting her pan back. Apparently there is a soup kitchen crisis and out of all the pans in her kitchen the only decent one she has is sitting in my kitchen." I knew it was a lie. If Mum really wanted her pan back she would have been on the phone the next day giving me a mouthful, spouting forth, telling me that, "If you couldn't be arsed finding time in your hectic schedule to return it, I'll just come around." Truth was, Mum was avoiding me as much as I was avoiding her. I could tell from George's voice that he'd had enough and was taking charge.

Then Neff started talking about the pan of bird food and afternoon sex, like she knew all about it – especially as she followed it up with a full head-back laugh, stopping Baby Bea in her food smashing tracks.

"Darling, it's not like you're the first to have afternoon sex," she finished up.

I could hear Steven in his man cave muttering or chuckling. Not sure which; not that I cared.

There is nothing more annoying, when you're annoyed, than happiness, and Neff's happiness was the pinnacle of annoying. Her happiness was like a stone in your shoe, like the constant riding of underpants up your arse and I wanted to swear.

"Did you feed the birds, then?" She beamed.

I asked ~~her~~ if she was trying to be funny, which she answered with an annoying, "Shh..." setting my teeth on edge. Being told to "Shh" in your own house can do that to any sane person and I was just about to tell her that when she said:

"Is that your mum?"

We listened as Mum and George pulled up the drive. There were a couple of car door slams, the roll of a wheelchair on gravel and muffled chastising from George.

"Mind and knock, and don't forget to yell," shouted Mum.

"For god sake, they're hardly going to be at it now. They know we're coming."

"You never know," Mum said, then shouted, "Anybody in?"

'I can see Baby Bea in the window," said George.

"We're just coming," shouted Mum. "Heading up the drive *now*."

"Jesus, Beatrice. Stop making a meal of things."

"Meal of things? You didn't walk in..." hissed Mum loudly; they were nearly at the door "...hearing your daughter..."

I could feel myself blush.

"It's not like we've never had sex in the afternoon before," snapped George.

"Don't shout," yelled Mum.

"You just told me to," George shouted back.

"Yes, but not about our *friggin'* sex life, there's no need to advertise it."

"I wasn't advertising, I was just *friggin'* saying."

Neff flung open–the door, radiating the sort of happiness that would make a hangover a million times worse. "Beatrice, I was just about to visit you," she said. "You've saved me the bother."

Mum pushed past in her wheelchair. "We all up and about then?" she shouted into the kitchen.

"Yeaaa, Nana," cooed Baby Bea.

George followed behind with his familiar eye rolling, planted a kiss on Baby Bea's head, pulled me to him with one of his warm bear hugs and then headed into Steven's man cave. Mum, avoiding me, circled the kitchen while I remained fixed at the sink, staring at a lone bird pecking at the grass. The men chuckled in the distance.

"Shall I make coffee?" said Neff.

The bird fluttered off.

Mum coughed a "good idea," while Baby Bea, gave up on carrot stick hammering and stretched her hands out for chair escape. When nobody noticed she began climbing, until Neff lifted her and plopped her onto Mum's lap. Mum's face softened as Neff continued to talk of coffee while wafting her bribery under Mum's nose.

I could see it was working, that Mum was weakening, it was pretty impressive to watch. She was even on the verge of opening the whisky, asking me for glasses when I felt something. It was something familiar, but something I hadn't felt for a long time. Something I never expected to feel again. I went to the loo.

My heart was pounding, too scared to think it was what it might be. It had been a month since I breastfed Baby Bea to sleep, an easy transition, but I was told not to expect anything too soon, and certainly not my periods returning.

Yet there it was, a proclamation of red: *your egg has landed, fired up your uterus, there's still some life in the ovaries yet, a bit of oestrogen...*I sat for ages on the toilet, listening as everyone piled into the kitchen. George and Steven were talking of lunch while Mum searched through my cupboards, moaning about the state of them.

"Sheryl?" shouted Mum. "Steven's making some soup for us all, where is that pan I left?"

I looked in the mirror and smiled at myself. I decided not to tell anybody, even Steven. Silly really, as Steven would know once we were in bed together. Yet later when he cuddled into me he said nothing about my period, just held me tighter, saying, "Baby Bea isn't a baby any more. Why don't we just call her Bea?"

I whispered a "yes" and turned to see him beaming straight back at me.

Chapter Forty-Six

THE AFFAIR

Sex after sixty is best with humour

Neff

I was in the restaurant taking an order for a takeaway from Lumpy when Ms Frasier walked in to pick up an order for Mr Finlay.

It was a Sunday night, the usual rush on take-aways had finished and I was feeling as flat as an empty paper bag, my LaLa feeling as distant as the South Pole. Not that anyone noticed. They were laughing yet again at The Lead's TikTok videos. You'd think after a month the whole Go Between saga would have died. I mean, it wasn't even that funny to begin with, yet there they were talking like it was the joke of the century, sniggering like schoolboys over a fart.

It was really beginning to grate. One more "those videos are pure genius" comments and I was ready to spit.

Hia and Tenzam were heading for Glasgow and Tenzam would not be back until late Tuesday. They were spending Monday at his cousin's, before Hia caught her plane home. Tenzam had even closed the restaurant and Tenzam *never* closed the restaurant.

I don't know why, but I felt down, like the end of Christmas Day when all the cooking and presents are done and there was just me and a flashing Christmas tree wondering, *what the fuck was all that about?* I don't do Christmas now, it's just another day to me and The Bag Lady.

We make one of our favorite dishes, have an early fire if it's dry or spend it inside.

The Bag Lady said now it was because I was at the beginning of an affair where you can't bear to be apart. "You're addicted to him," she said. "Once the sex becomes routine you'll be waving him off quite the thing."

I didn't have the heart to tell her she was talking bollocks.

How could she know what it's like to feel what I feel? What it's like to be in a world of Bangla conversations, a world you're not part of. A world of unfamiliar looks, songs, and memories. To lay in bed with a man while he talks on the phone and you haven't a clue what about. When Tenzam and Hia were together I felt old, foolish, and invisible, like I was intruding on something. As if I wasn't as important as I thought I was. I had happily included Tenzam into my whole world yet Hia seemed to exclude me and when I said anything to Tenzam he brushed me off, claiming I misunderstood. I wasn't experiencing withdrawals, I was experiencing doubt. Did he really care or was it just a fling?

Tenzam clumped upstairs, and Hia let out a laugh, silencing Ms Frasier and Lumpy.

"She's leaving tonight," said The Roadworks Man, as if I had no idea.

"She does have a family, *a* husband," I said, like I knew better than him.

"Aye but they're not close like those two, he'll miss her," said The Roadworks Man.

"Take no notice of him," advised Ms Frasier. "He makes up what he doesn't know."

Later that night when all was quiet, Tenzam came down to cash up. I made to leave and he held me close, looked into my eyes, then kissed me.

"Darling," he whispered in my ear.

Hia shouted for him.

"I better let you go." I gestured upstairs.

"She doesn't like flying," he said. "All the conferences she goes to and yet, she still fears being on a plane."

I slid my bag on my shoulder and headed for the door. "You better go to her then," I huffed.

He followed me to the door and made for another kiss – and then it happened.

Tenzam farted. Nothing loud or anything like that, just a small faint squeak, but it was definitely a fart.

———

That night I sat by The Bag Lady's fire in comfy warm clothes with a hot water bottle waiting for me in bed. I tucked into my first drink, constantly checking my phone for an "I made it safe and sound" text from Tenzam.

Friggin nothing.

I downed my second drink and checked again, this time cursing that there was still bugger all. By the time the bottle of wine was finished I was really cheesed off; there was still no text, not even a smiley face or a thumbs up. I mean how hard is it to let your partner know you're ok? How long does it take to text – a few seconds? As I drained my glass, my phone died.

"I thought we were soulmates," I muttered into the blank screen.

Betty and The Bag Lady, let out a series of inebriated tuts.

"No such thing as soulmates," said Betty.

"But if he cared wouldn't he text? Let me know he had arrived?"

The Bag Lady told me I had had too much to drink, that I should go to bed and charge up my phone.

"Can't be arsed," I told her, and opened another bottle. The thought of cuddling up to a hot water bottle can do that to a woman, make her linger, refuse to leave. Besides it was a mild, dry night, and I was pleasantly pissed, bordering on nostalgic. It had been ages since we sat together without waiting for Tenzam to arrive.

The Bag Lady and Betty were staring into a pretty decent fire like old timers in a Western reminiscing under the influence of a full moon. I had The Daughter of Ramses Two on my lap out for the count *and* purring, the four kittens were skipping about the place with at least another twenty minutes of play before they crashed into a ball of sleep and I had a hot water bottle to look forward to.

I was going nowhere.

Betty picked up the tomboy of the kittens, the one that jumped on the others and was always first at the cat bowl to eat. She ruffled his ginger ears. "Tell her about "Fabulous You", she said to The Bag Lady. She turned to me. "She worked there in the seventies."

The Bag Lady poked the fire.

"You know, when you had an affair with that man."

"Pff. Him." The Bag Lady looked at me. "You don't want to hear about that."

I topped up her glass. "Yes, I do."

Betty goaded her on.

"He *was* gorgeous," muttered The Bag Lady. "And the sex..." She sighed. "One position done to perfection like the perfect roast chicken."

"One position?" I looked at Betty.

"He was seeing the stiff-faced Lindsey when I started at "Fabulous You"," said The Bag Lady. "Her father owned the magazine and she did little apart from swan about the office ignoring us plebs. No one liked her and many said he was with her 'cause her father was rich. I just assumed that when we slept together he'd give her up."

"And did he...give her up?" I said.

"No, they got engaged," answered Betty.

"I told myself he wasn't happy with her, that he needed saving from the claws of such a hard woman. That he preferred me and my bedsit." She tossed a stick on the fire, sending the tiniest kitten scurrying. "Although he never stayed there. I kept thinking he would choose me over her, even when he bought her a ring, toasted her at their engagement party."

"You went to their engagement party?" I said.

"I told myself he looked sad, trapped, that we were soulmates. I sort of lived in hope, even when I received the wedding invitation."

"But you didn't go to that, did you?" I said.

"You were young," said Betty.

"And foolish. I mean, he never once talked of leaving her. He just kept meeting me in dark places, saying that this would be the last time and then doing it again." She paused for a minute. Then, "I remember sitting at the back of the church, clutching a stupid hymn book, my heart somersaulting while he was taking his vowels.

"On one side were all her rich friends and family done up like something out of "Dynasty". On his side was his family of four, a few friends and us office staff. We all clubbed in for a coffee maker as she was famous for striding in with a coffee just for him." She barked a laugh. "We thought he'd see the funny side."

"What happened?" I asked.

"When I saw him kiss her, I went numb, I felt nothing. I honestly believed he would turn around and shout, "I choose true love and a bedsit", like in one of those stupid romantic books. It took way too much alcohol to sink in. I got so drunk I fell asleep in the toilets, holding hands with the toilet holder. I woke the next day with no idea how I got home."

Betty and I waited, silent.

"He called me into the office a few days later. He had heard about the toilet holder incident and said I had to go. He said I had been heard shouting out sexual positions but I think he was just exaggerating – we only had one, and that was around the gear stick of my Ford Fiesta."

I looked at The Bag Lady; I couldn't believe what she was telling me, she sounded like a fool.

"He sent me to another paper where I wrote reviews for just about anything. It was a way better job. A few years later I saw them in Glasgow. I was doing a review in a hotel and they walked in with a baby. He didn't see me..." She paused again and poked the fire. "I'd liked to say he looked miserable, but he didn't. He looked comfortably rich like he was born to it, like he was used to folk running around after him."

I stared into the fire.

"The funny thing was I felt nothing, no sadness or regret, nothing. I guess the sex had blinded me to who he really was.' She looked at me with a smile. "What he could do in a car." The Bag Lady leaned down to stroke The Daughter of Ramses Two with a serene look. "It was so liberating to see someone who had broken your heart and be untouched. I was glad he didn't see me because I could enjoy my liberation without making small talk." She smiled. "And watching him act like a dickhead with the hotel staff was so reassuring." The Daughter of Ramses Two jumped onto her lap. "It was then I realised I liked being invisible, observing, and I decided to travel." She patted my thigh in a motherly fashion. "But that's another story."

Chapter Forty-Seven

THE DREAM

There is more to a snake than poison

Neff

Later that night I stared at the full moon peering into the bedroom window and pondered The Bag Lady's story. I wondered if it were true, was she ever that gullible? Or was she just trying to console, divert or shut me up? Give me a good story for my book.

I thought of writing everything down, perhaps recording it all on my phone, but then I realised that was charging downstairs, in the kitchen. I pulled the covers from my legs, sat up and then with an, "Oh shit," fell back on the bed and drifted into the sort of comatose sleep that a bottle and more of wine gives you.

I dreamt the sort of dream that had me sweating like I was in the middle of a hot flush.

I was standing in an office, writing the greatest pelvic story of all time in a belly dancing outfit that would give Cleopatra a run for her money. I had a snake around my neck, which for some strange reason was licking my ears as I typed on an old fashioned typewriter – mid hip circle. Hia appeared, dressed like Morticia in the Adams family, and hovering inches from the floor she, with a broad stroke of her arm and a head back crazy laugh, cleared my desk of papers, grabbed the snake, slung it around her neck and started cooking a curry.

Then Tenzam appeared and sniffed the curry like its aroma would make him high. I tried to grab his attention with a belly dance, but my hips refused to work, my feet were rooted to the ground and my arms were like lead. The Roadworks Man suddenly appeared and started to pack curries for carry-outs. And before I could shimmy, the three of them, spooning on a moped, rode off into the sunset with my friggin' snake billowing at the back like a flag.

I woke up in a sweat, with The Daughter of Rameses Two on my chest, breathing down my face with an "I'm starving" meow and a cold hot water bottle between my legs.

I pulled the hot water bottle out, eased myself out of bed and gingerly headed downstairs to the kitchen, grateful for cat biscuits. The thought of opening a tin of cat food had me retching at the thought.

Vague memories of trying to charge up my phone flashed back to me – rummaging through drawers in the kitchen, fumbling with the slow cooker lead, then shouting, "Wah lah," in the bathroom and plugging in my straighteners...

There it was: my phone charged and flashing perched in the coffee grounder.

Vowing to never drink again, I flicked onto my messages.

Sent in the middle of the night when I was wrestling with my straighteners was a message from Tenzam.

"Nit nit, darling. I miss you."

Chapter Forty-Eight

THE TANTRUM

There is nothing like a toddler tantrum to wreck a moment

Sheryl

A month after the kittens were born I took Bea to choose the kitten she wanted and she screamed the place down.

I could have killed Mum.

It was her idea to let Bea choose, her idea to wave a pile of kittens in front of Bea's nose and then take them away.

"If Bea is no longer a Baby Bea" she said "then she'll understand."

I did have my doubts, but Mum can be convincing and she was convinced that my wee Bea would understand that a cute kitten would be hers to take in a month or so – when it was old enough. Well, she didn't. She screamed as I dragged her to the car, and all the way back to Mum's house and even at Mum's Puss, who, with a "what have I done?" look shot out the door.

"Well, I never." Mum was briskly unwrapping a Tunnock's teacake.

"Don't give Bea chocolate," I snapped.

Mum thrust the teacake under her granddaughter's nose.

Bea, with a dark look at me, clutched the biscuit.

"You never screamed like that," said Mum. "And neither did your sister, or for that matter, her son."

Bea surveyed her favourite biscuit and let chocolate melt over her fingers.

"Yes, well, I was probably too scared to. And that son of Linsdey's is pussy- whipped."

"Don't use that language in my house," snapped Mum, sliding a biscuit my way.

"Every girl he brings home is as bossy as she is." I pushed the biscuit back.

"Still, you lot never screamed," Mum insisted.

"You never dangled a kitten in front of me and then took it away."

"Guess I'm smarter than you," said Mum.

"It was *your* friggin' idea."

"Don't shout, Sheryl. We've just got this daughter of yours quiet."

I looked at Bea, her mouth full of biscuit and her face covered in chocolate, and wondered, *how did she manage that so quickly?* She made to rub her nose, smearing even more chocolate. I dived to wipe, but Mum got there first, swiftly pulling her hidden Wet Wipes and over-taking my scrunched-up tissue faster than a rally driver past the post. It was one of the most annoying habits she had, apart from shit advice. I never knew where she hid the Wet Wipes but they were always inches from her just when she needed to pull them out like a magician.

"I should have listened to Steven," I muttered. "He said any kitten would do, that she didn't need to choose."

Mum tossed the Wet Wipe at the bin with expert aim and I tried not to look impressed.

"Funny enough, that's what Neff said and The Bag Lady as well."

Mum said nothing.

"There is nothing like a toddler tantrum to wreck a moment," I carried on, "and Bea threw one big time." Ignoring Mum's, "She's never done that with me," I told her about early that morning. How I walked into Neff's kitchen to find her over the sink, glass of water in one hand and a paracetamol in the other, nursing, according to her, "a hangover from hell." Her kitchen was in some state, like a blind drunk had been looking for a bottle opener and found the tin opener instead.

· · ·

"Oh, I forgot you were coming around," she'd said and attempted a half-hearted wave at Bea on my hip. "You sure it's a good idea her choosing a kitten? She might want to, you know, take it home with her?"

"Mum says she's old enough to understand," I'd said.

"Pff, well, if your Mum says..."

We headed out to her garden where Betty and The Bag Lady were also looking fragile. Apparently, Tenzam was away in Glasgow for some family thing and the three women had made a night of it.

The Bag Lady, perched on her log seat, was sipping tea with a pinched face like she was forcing it down. Betty was sitting cross-legged at the tent entrance rubbing her head, and she also tried a feeble wave at Bea.

"You sure this is a good idea?" The Bag Lady coughed. "She might want...to... you know."

"Sheryl's mum says it'll be ok," shouted Neff. She grimaced, and copied Betty in rubbing her forehead.

"Well if *she* says it's ok" murmured Betty.

Bea turned to Betty, spied The Daughter of Ramses Two behind her in the tent and with a quick scramble from my hips she was there, inches from the cat's bed.

'Too late now," muttered Neff.

I followed inside. Bea squatting beside The Daughter of Ramses Two was transfixed, she reached to touch the tiny bundles of fur then withdrew. She had never seen kittens before.

The Daughter of Ramses Two stood up with a prolonged stretch then, kneading the rug beneath her, let out a half meow/half purr to her four kittens. There were three black and one ginger, rolling and flopping under their mother, letting out the occasional baby meows.

Bea didn't move. I sat next to her. She snuggled in as The Daughter of Ramses Two began to groom her brood with her tongue.

Prrrrr....

Betty appeared beside me. "The ginger is male," she whispered. "The others are female."

Prrrrr....

Bea looked up at me, her face beaming, then turned straight back to watch them.

Neff and The Bag Lady were still outside, talking about the night before, how much wine they had had and the mess Neff woke too.

"Never try to charge your phone when you see double," she said.

The Bag Lady chuckled then stopped to cough.

"Tenzam did text though," said Neff.

"Told you," spluttered The Bag Lady.

"I know, I was a complete twat."

"We've all been there," said The Bag Lady. She peered into the tent. "You alright..." She stopped. "Awwww."

"You chosen yet?" Neff yelled from outside. "You get first pick." She peered in. "Awww."

The Bag Lady and Neff joined us in silence. The baby meows of the kittens filled the tent. Bea stretched out her hand to touch the ginger kitten, who nuzzled her finger then made to swipe it. Bea pulled away, then reached out again.

"Would you like the ginger one?" I asked her.

"And that was your first mistake," muttered Mum now.

I looked at her. "*You* told me to ask her."

"You should have just watched, see which one she went for."

"Which is what I did," I said.

"But then you *leave*, without a word. You *surprise* her in a few weeks."

Unbelievable.

Bea looked for another biscuit, and Mum pulled one from the tin. This time she unwrapped with a dance of her hands.

Bea chuckled. She stretched out for the biscuit.

"Don't you think one is enough?" I said.

"Do you ever feed this child?" Mum gave Bea a gooey smile.

"Of course I friggin' do."

"Don't swear, Sheryl." Mum reversed her wheelchair to the fridge. She pulled out a bottle of something way too orange to be natural and filled Bea's beaker cup.

"Mum that stuff is full of chemicals, it probably glows in the dark."

"Nonsense, this *stuff* never hurt you."

"What are you talking about? There was none of that fluorescent fluid years ago."

"Well, that son of Lindsey's drank it, and look at him."

"Lindsey never used that *stuff.* She's as organic as compost."

Mum was silent.

"It's full of sugar. You've virtually given my child a whole packet of teacakes and a bucket of sugar juice."

"A little bit of what you fancy does you good," said Mum – yet again. She was always saying that, and for some reason it really got on my nerves. I must have looked pissed because Mum started to ask me what was wrong, why was I in such a mood. "Anyone would think it was that time of the month," she snapped.

I made to wipe Bea's face.

Bea pushed me away.

Mum handed Bea's cup to her with a "Here, pet." Then she added, "I'm sorry. I forgot. That was tactless of me."

"Actually, it is," I said.

She looked at me. "Tactless?"

"No..." I hadn't wanted to tell her. I didn't want to tell anyone in case my period was a one off, but when I saw her face I was glad I did. She looked so happy for me.

"So there's hope? You may have another?"

I nodded. "We can but try."

"Well," she said with a crisp wipe about Bea's lips. "Let's hope you learn from your mistakes, and not repeat them."

Friggin' hell, I thought. *Friggin' bleeding hell.*

Chapter Forty-Nine

THE NEW ADDITION

Letting go is not the same as giving up, even though it feels like it

Sheryl

A month and no visits to Mum later I headed around to Neff's to pick up Bea's kitten. This time I was doing it my way and Mum could shove her advice up her jumper; we even sourced another cat carrier rather than borrow hers.

I don't know who was more excited, me or Steven; we hadn't told Bea and couldn't wait to see her face. I slipped out with our bargain-priced cat carrier while Steven distracted Bea. Not that she needed it – she was busy with her new box of crayons, tossing them on the floor.

I arrived to meet Finlay's daughter on the drive, with Damian, her son, clutching an "I have more money than sense" cat carrier with two meowing cats inside. She stopped to talk, while Damian, barely tall enough to carry the carrier marched with purpose to the car.

"He can't wait," she said. "He wanted to come weeks ago and choose, but I told him to wait, it would only upset him to leave without them."

I said nothing.

"Ms Frasier told her about the cats, and we jumped at the chance," she said. "My son is animal mad, and awfully fond of Ms Frasier, loves her Australian stories. What that woman doesn't know..." She sighed.

I didn't have the heart to argue, to say, "Just wait till she gets her hands on *your* garden, starts playing monopoly with *your* time, ear bashing you to death."

"She's a god send," Finlay's daughter went on. "My father is a new man, forgotten all about his prostate – never mentions it *and* Ms Frasier has taken over his garden. He's delighted–"

"Mum!" shouted Damian.

"Just coming." The daughter waved. "It was a dump, on account of his "dodgy everything"". Not now. The garden is pure organic." She laughed. "He's brought two compost bins and is obsessed with filling them."

"Mum!"

The daughter waved again at her son. "Even brought a new wheelbarrow. He sits outside directing her while she arranges his gnomes."

"Mum! They're wanting food."

"Not that I'm a gnome person, but if it keeps him happy..." She headed for the car.

"Ms Frasier's a miracle worker," she yelled with a hearty a jump into the car.

"She just texted," Damian called. "She says she's got that *special* kitten milk."

"See what I mean?" The daughter beamed at me and with yet another quick wave drove off.

I had no idea about Ms Frasier and Mr Finlay as I had been avoiding Mum, but I have to say nothing cheers the soul like a romance story, especially when I had Bea at home with no idea what was coming her way.

I headed into the garden with a Christmas morning joy.

The Bag Lady and Betty were looking miserable, while Neff was shouting, "This is why I told you not to give them names."

"Sounds like Ms Frasier and Finlay are an item," I said attempting to spread the love.

"Pff," said Neff. 'I hardly see her now."

"They are like that," grumbled The Bag Lady with a crossed finger gesture.

"She said they spend all their time in Finlay's garden."

"Worse than Neff and her man," said The Bag Lady.

Neff threw her a glare.

"Don't like the look of that Damien," muttered Betty.

"He'll be fine," snapped Neff.

"And when they're not in the garden," I said, "they're cracking puns in shops. I was in the chemist the other day..."

"Or posting on Twitter," huffed The Bag Lady.

Twitter? I had no idea The Bag Lady knew about Twitter, it's not like she spends her days in the tent with a laptop or an iPad.

"I heard he's joined the Community Garden Project," said Neff. "Become a judge."

"Why he's a judge is beyond me," said The Bag Lady. "His garden is a bombsite, needs more than the Ms Frasier treatment, it needs a friggin' weapon of mass destruction."

Neff handed me a mug of coffee. "I went over to finish her recordings and there was Finlay hunched over like a turtle and her searching for the Deep Heat. He tried to help and did his back in."

"That woman loves to get her hands dirty." The Bag Lady tossed the remains from her mug onto the fire embers.

"Damien changed their names." Betty sighed. "The kittens. That's not a good sign."

The Bag Lady nodded sagely.

"I told you," snapped Neff, "we can't keep all of them."

I stared down at the kittens. "Where's the ginger one?"

"Ms Frasier took it," said The Bag Lady.

"I thought that one was Bea's?" I said.

"She took it for Mr Finlay's daughter apparently she is partial to a bit of ginger," said Betty.

"But we agreed," I said.

"I told you it was a bad idea," said The Bag Lady to Neff.

"She can be pretty persuasive," said Neff.

"And what Bea wants doesn't matter?" I huffed.

"She didn't shut up, *and* she was taking two." Neff looked apologetic.

Betty with a nod at Neff whispered to me, "She's love sick, all gaga."

"I am not." Neff scowled. "We are now on farting terms."

"We did agree on the ginger one. You should have..." I stopped. "Farting terms?"

"Yes, you know when you let your guard down, stop wearing lipstick in bed."

"I never wore lipstick in bed," I said.

"That's because you're not sixty. Once you're sixty it takes a while to you know, show the real face."

"Just as well," said Betty. "We pretty much live on curries, even The daughter of Ramses Two is partial to the odd bit of chicken Jalfrezi; she has the wind of a pregnant cow." She sniffed. "Woke the ginger one once."

"Don't get me started." The Bag Lady blew her nose.

I looked from one kitten to the other. One was all black and a bit scraggy, the other had a bow-tie white spot under her chin and matching white paws. She was definitely the cutest. I watched her getting a serious grooming from her mother. *Bea would love her*.

"You choose, and we'll keep the other," said Neff, "although it looks like the one with the white paws would like to stay."

"She does love a bit of korma." Betty sighed.

"Are you telling me to take the all-black one?"

"Well, no," said Neff. "But the all-black is very independent...look at her."

The all-black kitten, mid-rolling about the fire embers, stopped to eyeball me.

"Awww," muttered Betty.

The kitten jumped and skipped towards my feet, stopped at my toes and looked up with "pick me" eyes.

"It's like she has chosen you," said The Bag Lady.

'But feel free...." muttered Neff. She wiped her eye; I thought I saw a tear, which threw me a bit, she's never been big on children or anything little. I mean she's fond enough of Bea but one sniffly nose, one whiff of a smelly nappy, one hint of a tantrum and she is off. Now, Neff sat by The Daughter of Ramses Two with a soft look, as he Daughter of Rameses Two snuggled around the bow-tie kitten with a purr.

The all-black cat made a playful pounce at my foot. I tickled her wee belly. *Did I really have a choice?*

When I appeared with the all-black cat in the carrier, Bea was busy destroying a colouring book with rapid scribbling, and Steven was reading. Neither looked up, even when I plonked the carrier on the ground.

Meow squeaked All-Black.

Bea dropped her pen.

Steven closed his book.

Meow meow....

Bea scrambled to the carrier, I opened its door, All-Black peered out and spied Bea.

Meow. Bea stretched her hand out to the kitten. All-Black tentatively sniffed it, and Bea, who normally went at things like, to quote Mum, "a bull in a china shop" waited, crossed-legged and transfixed. The kitten moved towards her, rubbed along her side, scrambled over her knee and fell into her lap.

Bea looked up at me with a smile, then gently tapped All-Black's head.

Chapter Fifty

THE WAKE

There is no sweetness in parting—only sorrow

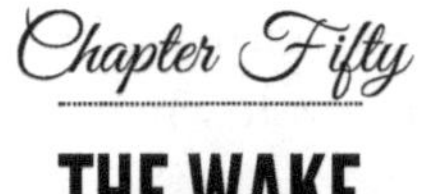

Neff

That night Tenzam listened as he always did while I rabbited on about the kittens.

We were in bed, talking in the dark, him cuddling – hoping for something more – and me stalling. I didn't feel like the full bhoona, the whole enchilada of lovemaking, I wanted a hug and a listening ear and Tenzam was smart enough to read me. Watching the kittens go was not an easy thing to do and The Bag Lady and Betty moaning about it didn't help.

The Bag Lady and Betty, who both lived by the "letting go" mantra, struggled with giving up the kittens. They didn't want to let go either and kept putting Sheryl and Ms Frasier off, spending their days in the tent cooing and aahing – although they did draw the line at wailing.

I couldn't believe how attached we had all become. I loved the names Betty gave them, not that I said anything, in fact I scorned Betty for naming them.

"You'll just get attached," I said. Like we hadn't already.

"Can we not keep one," said Betty, "for the mother's sake?"

I wanted to keep them all.

In the end the kittens decided: the ginger kitten jumped straight into Ms Frasier's arms and the one I loved the most chose Sheryl. At least the two with Damian could be together, I told myself, not that it helped. After the three kittens were gone it was like a wake.

Tenzam appeared later that night and asked who'd died? Or was someone sick? And when we told him he looked confused. He didn't really "get" pets. Cats and dogs were just scraggy animals in the streets where he came from, animals that children teased and tormented, tossed water at when they were procreating. Tenzam's world was a tough world, and sometimes I could see it in his face. It was probably due to his parents dying when he was thirteen. Hia was three at the time and looked at Tenzam as a father figure ever since. Not that that made it easier for me to deal with...I found their bond almost on a par with infidelity but I was learning to, well, swallow my fears whole.

Tenzam had talked of his past many times: how an aunt moved in and took care of them; how she was a widow with a small baby boy and little money; how Tenzam's large family home was, as he put it "an answer to her prays". He said his parents were well off and his aunt was considered by the family to be a trustworthy woman. He said she did her best to use his parents' money wisely and educated Tenzam, Hia and their cousin. She had even found a husband for Hia, arranged her marriage. And now it seems she had found a wife for his cousin, the aunt's son.

"Did she not arrange a wife for you, then?" I said.

He shook his head. "I want to make money first."

I stared at him. His answer shocked me.

"Before I met you," he quickly added.

I rolled over in a huff...

Tenzam had me on my toes all the time, he was constantly surprising me. At times I was philosophical about the whole thing, other times I raged by The Bag Lady's fire – usually under the influence of a wine of two – then I'd calm down, adjust yet again, but an arranged marriage was something else.

"You hungry?" he asked now.

"I'm ok."

"Biscuit, maybe?"

"Not just now," I muttered into my pillow.

"Something hot?"

I didn't answer.

"Chips?"

I turned to face him. "Chips? Now?"

"Just teasing." He laughed "You are very quiet tonight."

"Am I?"

I wanted to tell him I didn't believe him, that I thought he was lying, hiding things from me, but instead I told him I was thinking about the kittens.

"Shall I go away?" he said not moving.

"Go away, in the middle of the night?"

He threw me his best "just teasing" smile.

I pulled out my phone and played Sheryl's recordings of Bea and the kitten, my heart heavy with sadness. "She's called her kitten All-Black," I muttered.

Tenzam stared at the video. "I have no plans to marry," he said. "Meeting you has changed everything."

I swallowed back a tear; sometimes it was hard to believed him. He had a way of springing things on me like he had just made them up. I flicked through my messages and found another video of Damian and his two kittens. "Life is all about letting go." I sighed.

Tenzam made to hug me. I made to push him away; he hugged me harder.

"But I do not want to let you go," he whispered.

Chapter Fifty-One

THE GARDEN PROJECT

A smart person loves the sound of silence

Sheryl

The Red Cross Shop won the Garden Project trophy – not that anyone was surprised.

In fact so sure was Helen that she made a shelf behind the shop counter for the trophy, free of charge.

"Let's call it a donation to a good cause," she said and left with a complimentary bag of someone's unwanted toiletries.

A picture of Ms Frasier handing the trophy over was on the front page of the local paper, along with a centrefold spread and more pictures. She-who-lives-to-Moan was the only volunteer not in the photos. An old "rumbling" tooth abscess flared up the very day Ms Frasier's "Congratulations, you have won", letter arrived at the shop and she was having the "extraction from hell" while the others posed for the photographer. Neff called it karma, claiming the whole sorry scenario would give She-who-lives-to-Moan something new to moan about. I told her she didn't mean it, that she wouldn't wish a tooth abscess on anyone, that she was still hurting from the kittens leaving. Neff, of course, denied it, claiming it was all part of her "letting go" mantra, but I had seen the look in her eyes when All-Black left.

The volunteers also won a free fish supper, care of Gordon the chippy, who wanted to show "no hard feelings". They posed again for the local paper after that, this time with She-who-lives-to-Moan, despite her swollen jaw. She, clutching her free battered sausage supper (she was allergic to haddock) posed on her good side, with the sort of lopsided grin that made her look drunk.

Jason the fishmonger, not to be out done, offered them a free smoked kipper, which led to another centre page spread; this time She-who-lives-to-Moan doing a full frontal I'm not drunk grin, her jaw no longer swollen.

Afterwards they celebrated at The Taj. Neff was a bit sniffy as she wasn't needed.

Tenzam's cousin had appeared and according to Neff, he took over like an interfering mother-in-law. She said she was glad to leave, that she was fed up with She-who-lives-to-Moan and her crowing. "Let that know-it-all cousin deal with her," she huffed.

But I could read Neff's face like a shopping list. She was as pissed as Mum when someone mentioned her wheelchair, and just as bad at hiding it.

Chapter Fifty-Two

MAVIS

Adjusting to change is as easy as adjusting a bra in situ

Neff

Ms Frasier had changed, her friendship with Finlay seemed to have curbed her tongue. She was quieter, looked content, like she was mulling things over, and was now too busy to finish our interviews.

Mavis said that all Ms Frasier's talk of sex in other places was an exaggeration, that she had never been anywhere and the likelihood of her having it off with Finlay was as probable as Tenzam and I having a baby, which I thought was a bit low. Mavis was standing in The Taj at the time with no intention of ordering, but rather asking me if I was ever going to interview *her* for my book.

"Not that I'm bothered," she said.

Lumpy looked at me with a "she is" look.

"It's just that if you are, you need to let me know, as Lumpy and I will be on holiday soon."

"Let's make it this week," I said as The Chef appeared from behind, silent, like a shadow. He threw me a strange look; I gave him a half-hearted smile. I was used to weird looks from The Chef, which I put down to his poor English. He said little to me but spoke sermons to Tenzam in Bangla, and when Tenzam translated, the sermon became a mere sentence of bugger all.

I carried on shuffling things about behind the till like I was inundated with orders when Tenzam walked through the kitchen with his cousin in toe. I greeted them with a warm smile as he introduced me. I had heard a lot about the cousin and despite having no idea he was due to arrive I acted like I did, until he stood on *my* side of the counter and fingered *my* pad.

Then I began to feel apprehensive – yet again.

"My sister is needing help," said Tenzam.

I stared at the till, with a sigh.

"She wants me to help my cousin."

"Oh?" I said, throwing a smile the cousin's way.

He smiled back then headed into the kitchen clutching *my* pad, bursting into a Bangla conversation with The Chef. The Chef chuckled. The cousin roared with laughter, Tenzam made to join, caught my eye and stopped.

"He is going to work here," Tenzam said.

I stopped, my face hot with embarrassment. Mavis and Lumpy had a way of watching that made me feel like a child and it was pointless even pretending I knew.

"Does that mean you don't need me?"

His cousin shouted at Tenzam in Bangla.

"In a minute," Tenzam shouted back, also in Bangla.

"But what about the booking tonight?" I said. "The Garden Project team? You know how Ms Frasier gets…"

The cousin appeared from the kitchen. "I know what to do."

"Does he?" I asked Tenzam.

"I have been working in our Glasgow restaurant for months," the cousin said.

"Why don't you leave early?" Tenzam said to me.

Mavis and Lumpy looked from me to Tenzam.

Tenzam coughed. "…only if you want, that is."

I looked from Mavis to Lumpy then at Tenzam, wondering if trying to adjust to his ways was worth all the bloody hard work when he still managed to knock me off balance.

Let go I told myself, and almost managed it. "I suppose I could go home," I muttered. "Finish off that chapter I'm on. Make way for you, Mavis." I attempted a laugh. I headed for the door, stopped, looked at Tenzam. "Will I see you later?"

"Of course," he said with an uncomfortable laugh.

Chapter Fifty-Three

THE COUSIN

A sandwich is never as good as a roll no matter how hard to tell yourself it is

Sheryl

I was in the bathroom contemplating my hairy legs and whether I could go another day without a shave when I caught sight of my toenails. I hadn't looked at them for a while and it still wasn't pretty. I stared closer. *Did I see some new growth...some hope?*

Steven appeared. "All's quiet on the western front." He laughed, wrapped his arm around my waist and kissed my neck. "She's out for the count." Steven never bothered about the state of my legs, or for that matter my toenails, and as it was raining for the next few days I figured who would see my legs?

Fuck it, I thought and followed him to bed.

All I had to do was turn off the light, light a candle, and even I wouldn't see when we were making love.

———

Neff

That night Tenzam appeared later than usual and looking sheepish. He had something on his mind and I didn't want to ask.

I was sitting by the fire, with The Bag Lady and Betty, watching

The Daughter of Ramses Two stroll from one corner of the hot tub, to the other with perfect balance. Like she was showing off, shouting look at me, still got it, still able to sashay on a tight rope, despite all those kittens.

The hot tub was covered up on account of Betty having shingles and The Bag Lady didn't want to torment her.

"I will wait until the all clear, when you can hop in with me," she said without even one thought of me.

Truth was they had run out of dope...and without a spliff, the run from the tent to the hot tub was just too damn cold.

The kitten, now named Spectre appeared from nowhere as Tenzam took a seat.

Spectre jumped up onto the hot tub and with her tiny tail upright like a flag made to follow her mother.

I asked Tenzam if there was anything wrong.

"Wrong?" he said. "No, very quiet night, just as well you went home. Although Ms Frasier polished off most of the wine. Finlay's daughter was their taxi."

I waited.

The Roadworks Man had already filled me in, claiming Ms Frasier had "talked for Britain, Europe and the whole bleeding world," as the daughter stood there waiting for her to finish and asking, "Is she always this mouthy."

The kitten skidded; there had been a downpour and the sides of the hot tub were slippery. The Bag Lady and Betty took her inside the teepee to dry.

Tenzam turned to me. "My cousin is ready to run the restaurant."

"Oh?"

"His wife arrived tonight."

"I see."

"I will leave him here and go to the Glasgow restaurant tomorrow."

"Oh."

"Don't be mad, darling, we can still see each other."

Chapter Fifty-Four

GONE

Some relationship are like vegan cheese, looks the part until you bite into it

Neff

When Tenzam left I went into the Red Cross shop and pondered over the toiletries. I knew he was going even before he said it. I knew as soon as I saw him, and when he told me I tried my best to accept it, to convince myself I felt a sense of relief. I don't know why, I guess a part of me wanted the separation over and done with.

"A great sex memory is a good thing and not many have that," The Bag Lady said more than friggin' once. In fact, she said it so many times I wanted to punch her.

I wanted more than a memory, I wanted a happy ending and I thought I had it, but it had come and gone quicker than dishwater down a plug hole, slipping through my fingers like egg white.

My affair with Tenzam had me writing my heart out, reaching new pinnacles of creativity. The obsessive highs and confused lows of a love struck sixty-something, feeling fabulous – then forgotten; delicious – then fearful. I had written it all down, and now I had to move on. Not that I was ready.

I picked up a lavender soap, and thought, *Bugger this I'm going to buy myself some shit hot perfume.*

As I entered the chemist Finlay was there, seated by the foot fungal creams, his daughter beside him looking cheesed off.

The chemist slid his prescription onto the counter.

"At my age it's a carry-out." Finlay winked at me.

His daughter rolled her eyes.

"For me it's a tube of lubricant," boomed Ms Frasier from behind the dental stand.

His daughter sighed. "What are you doing here?"

"Bunions, luv," said Ms Frasier.

"The size of a molehill," said Finlay. "Makes massage so much more..." He looked at his daughter.

'Spit it out, Dad." She sighed.

"....challenging." Finlay chuckled.

The chemist closed the till with a laugh. Ms Frasier nearly wet herself, cackling, while the daughter, stony-faced, headed for the door.

Finlay caught my eye. "My work here is done," he said, sending his daughter into a series of tuts.

One bottle of perfume and matching soap later I arrived home to find The Bag Lady building the largest fire ever. Betty's shingles were past the catchable stage and as there was no dope to make the run from the tent to the hot tub bearable The Bag Lady figured a large fire would.

I watched through the kitchen window as she built with meticulous intent, fussing over the right kindling, clearing the odd shrub, dragging wood up from the loch. She looked so absorbed. I poured a coffee as The Bag Lady arranged her logs in a perfect pyramid, occasionally stopping to stroked the kitten. I wouldn't say I was content, that I was skipping about the place at the thought of a fire or writing a story, but at least I had someone to make a coffee for. And maybe one day, when I walked into the chemist to hear Finlay's jokes I would laugh out loud again.

Sheryl

The Bag Lady had built a huge bonfire and Neff had asked me around to see it. She said she was getting back to her belly dancing roots and wanted me to join her.

"Let's dance around the fire," she said.

It had been a long time since she had hip circled, let alone waffled on about the magic of it and I could see her heart wasn't in it. I didn't know what else to say, Tenzam and Neff had seemed so happy, I never thought he'd leave.

I asked her how her book was going. "Steven says you're a natural."

"Really?"

"Yes, he says you captured Ms Frasier in a way he thought impossible. And you've surprised Mum. She thinks you the next Alistair MacLean...or was it Alexander McCall Smith?"

Neff stopped mid hip circle, flustered like she wasn't used to compliments, like it was the last thing she expected.

"I told you that too," said The Bag Lady.

Neff stared at the fire.

"No you didn't," said Betty. "You called it Jackie Collins poignant."

"Jackie Collins?" The Bag Lady looked at Neff. "She's a genius."

Still Neff didn't answer, despite the fact that she hated Jackie Collins, like she hated most romantic books. "I write of real women," she was always announcing. "Warts, dried up fanny's and all," which I had to admit had most of us pulling faces.

Neff sat on a log. "It's the end of an era." She sighed. "The end of me coming home smelling of spices."

"He's only gone to Glasgow," said The Bag Lady.

Neff topped up her glass. "The lust has turned to friendship," she proclaimed like she was quoting Shakespeare, "the sex to repeat performances – comfortable like a worn out slipper..."

"It's a hour drive away," muttered The Bag Lady. "Free on the bus."

"...or an old bra," said Neff. She looked at me. "I guess he had had enough"

"Who are you kidding?" said Betty. "It takes years to get to that stage, years of sleeping together, year of him warming up the bed with farts, and you're so used to it you don't even notice."

"He did say you could visit," The Bag Lady reminded her.

"Years of his socks, your legs flaying about the bed, him thinking he's doing you a big favour when all you really want is for him to make you a good cup of tea," said Betty.

"And he would come and see you." The Bag Lady gave a 'shut it' look to Betty.

"And I'm knackered trying to keep everything tip top for a young man," said Neff unconvincingly. "Let's toast to moving on." She topped up our glasses. "To greater adventures..."Neff turned to me "...and if I say it often enough I will damn well believe it. Not that I would tell anyone but you."

EPILOGUE

Neff

I decided that along with decent perfume I needed a decent haircut and so I found a hairdresser near Tenzam's Glasgow restaurant, not that I told anyone. I sat on the bus, a little nervous, jumped off in a mixture of apprehension, then walked into the restaurant.

In the last few days I had come to terms with being single, that odd bit of sex with a friend had it perks, and sleeping on my own gave me energy, time for other things.

Sheryl wants another baby and needs me to help with her pelvic moves; Mavis's stories keep me more than friggin' busy, and Ms Frasier having re-read The Bag Lady's scrapbook more time than I've had curries wants me look up Beryl. She said Beryl is a great story in the making, but I think it's pure nosiness. I mean, she is worse than The Roadworks Man, who I've heard, now hangs out at the Chinese takeaway.

It was lunchtime, and the restaurant was empty; I took a seat by the window.

Tenzam appeared in black and when he saw me his face lit up. "Why did you take so long?" he said. "I have missed you."

"I thought you left for good," I told him, "that it was over..." I stopped just shy of saying, *that I had lost you to your family*. Tenzam's sweet smile stopped me.

"Did you not get my texts."

"Well, yes, but they were hardly helpful. "I'm safe and sound', is not the same as "I still love you", is it?"

"But I do," he said, and before I could answer, say, "You need to tell me that more often," he launched into a spiel about his family.

Here we go I thought, *some convoluted long-winded explanation that will lead me down a garden path that no sane woman could fathom.*

He stopped mid-sentence. "Whisky?"

I looked at him.

"You're not going back till tomorrow, are you?"

———

Sheryl

That night Steven and I watched as Bea and All-Black skidded about the floor.

Bea and I had spent the afternoon at Mum's, watching her and her ~~knew~~ power sprayer which she thought was brilliant, until it sent her gnomes flying across the yard.

Puss was missing for hours and eventually I found her curled up under the kitchen sink, a shivering ball of wet.

I was heading home with a fish and chips supper when I caught sight of Neff bouncing off the Glasgow bus like something out of Sex in the City. Sporting a jaw-dropping new haircut and a glow about her like she had overdosed on oestrogen, she waved at me like she hadn't seen me for months. She said she had found a great hairdresser, and someone that massaged her to heaven and back, and was now hot on the trail to finding the infamous Beryl of The Bag Lady's scrapbook. She didn't even comment about my drowned-rat hairstyle (care of Mum's power hose) but with a coo at Bea, she literally skipped to her car.

"What a turnaround," I said to Steven. "She is really putting a brave face on things."

He looked at my hair and ruffled it,.

"I asked her about the hairdresser, "I said, "but she said she was fully booked up to Christmas and beyond."

Steven laughed. 'You don't need a hairdresser. You have the hair of that Jason guy in Game Of Throne."

I'm sure there was a compliment in there.

That night I painted more fungus cream on my toenails while listening to Steven read Bea to sleep. There were times when I ached for another baby, when I felt empty at the thought that my period would stop, that it was all just a false alarm.

I was blowing my almost-new toenail dry, when from nowhere All-Black appeared, stumbling to a stop at my feet. She sniffed my toe, pulled back with a sneeze, then ran her body along my thigh.

I stroked her, thinking about Neff's great day in Glasgow.

How lucky was I?

I had the sort of heaven and back massage on tap, reading Bea to sleep next door.

And I didn't have to pay a penny.

~

Fancy something funny but different? Then why not try ***A Dame Called Derek?***
A Scottish comedy with crazy characters, on sale at your favourite store
Or if you want to try before you buy keep reading for an excerpt

A hard-on is only as good as the hand that holds it

George, along with the rest of the cast, watched in awkward silence as Derek tried to capture the essence of Rod Stewart. With an improvised tap dance, he limped and stuttered . . .

"Do ya think I'm sexy . . ."

George, tight-lipped, used all his energy to suppress a militant yell involving a fair amount of swearing.

George had spent years ordering men around in the army and had retired with a strong urge to control. When asked to direct the panto players, he jumped at the chance and ran them like a regiment. George had "done" many pantos in his day; granted it was back in the army days when cars had four gears and seat belts were optional, but he knew his stuff and a lousy act when he saw it.

Derek stuttered, *"Come on . . . su-su-sugar . . ."*

"Derek," said George through clenched teeth, "I thought we agreed to give the tap-dancing a miss this year."

Derek was about to say "the kids love it" when his plum round body overbalanced, taking the stage curtains with him on the way down.

———

Charlie fumbled into bed. Francis, his wife, didn't move.

"You'll never guess," said Charlie.

Francis mumbled into her pillow.

Charlie looked at her back. Was she awake? He took a gamble and began to tell her about Derek's Rod Stewart.

Francis rolled over and pushed the blanket back, exposing Charlie's leg to the cold. She rose from the bed and, with a grunt, swung her legs over the side.

Charlie watched his wife stumble into the wardrobe, mutter something medical, and then hobble to the bathroom.

Charlie pulled out his notebook and wrote: *scrap Rod Stewart . . .*

Francis came back from the bathroom with a glass of water.

A nipple peeked through one of the many holes in her "Frankie Says Relax" T-shirt. In the half-light of his lamp, Charlie stopped to admire.

He watched her bare legs move under the covers. He loved her legs. Over the years her lean figure had become almost androgynous, except for her legs. Watching her bare legs slip into sling-back sandals was one of the highlights of the summer.

Charlie slid his hand across to her thigh; Francis pushed his hand away and rolled over with a small snort. He looked back at his page; the inspiration had gone and so had his hard-on.

———

Charlie met Francis twenty years ago. She had bought her first hairdressing salon and was celebrating with a few vodkas and "The Rivers of Babylon" on the jukebox. It was Charlie's first day as a barman.

Charlie made eye contact with a slim woman with dark eyelashes. She smiled at him and his tray of vodka cocktails crashed to the floor. Her slender legs didn't move an inch as he mopped up the spillage by her feet; instead her dress inched higher. He looked up, caught a flash of suspenders, and dropped the tray again. Francis picked up the glass with her toe and slid it effortlessly onto his tray.

Francis was a woman who knew what she wanted. She seduced

Charlie and he didn't know what hit him. Two sets of twins and four salons later, Francis had turned from a flexible-toed seductress to a volatile, single-minded pain in the arse with an ego the size of the Himalayas and a determination that crushed whatever lay in her path.

Francis, like George, was used to getting her own way.

****

At your favourite store

A NOTE FROM THE AUTHOR

I hope you enjoyed Neff and Sheryl's latest story; inspired by the joys of living apart from the one you love and a decent bout of foot fungus. *The Other Side Of Yes* is the sixth book in the Bellydancing and Beyond Series, stand alone comedies about a group of women who danced with the great Nefertiti.

Sheryl's Last Stand is the first book in the series, if you haven't read her yet, why not give her a go and find out how it all started.

You can find me and my groovy blogs at

www.kerrienoor.com

Like me at

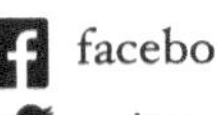 facebook.com/kerrienoorwriter

 twitter.com/kezzamac

 instagram.com/kerrienoor

The Other Side Of Yes

First edition. 29th June 2023.
Copyright © 2023 Kerrie Noor.
Written by Kerrie Noor.